ZONES OF CHAOS

Other titles by Mick Farren:

Fiction:
Conflagration
Kindling
Underland
More Than Mortal
Darklost
Jim Morrison's Adventures in the Afterlife
Back From Hell
The Time of Feasting
Necrom
Mars - The Red Planet
The Last Stand of the DNA Cowboys
The Armageddon Crazy
Exit Funtopia (aka *The Long Orbit*)
Their Masters' War
CORP*S*E (aka *Vickers*)
Protectorate
The Song of Phaid The Gambler
The Feelies
The DNA CowboysTrilogy
The Tale of Willy's Rats
The Texts of Festival

Non-fiction:
Who's Watching You?: The Chilling Truth about the State, Surveillance and Personal Freedom (With John Gibb)
Give The Anarchist A Cigarette
Conspiracies, Lies And Hidden Agendas
The CIA Files
The Hitchhiker's Guide to Elvis
Watch Out Kids

ZONES OF CHAOS

Poetry, Prose, Essays, Lyrics,
Commentary, and Short Fiction
by Mick Farren

Introduction by
Michael Moorcock

RED SNAKE
PRESS
SAN FRANCISCO

First Edition

ISBN 978-0-9729942-0-0

Red Snake Press
San Francisco, CA
www.redsnakepress.com

This collection is for my mother Gwendoline, who certainly pointed me towards the backroads of chaos.

Contents

ALTERNATIVE ACID

by Michael Moorcock

It's something of a consoling thought that Mick Farren and I go back over thirty years; him an "underground" editor of *International Times* (as *IT* was originally called) and front man for the Pink Fairies, me editing *New Worlds* and, when Bob Calvert was indisposed, fronting for Hawkwind. Both bands would sometimes combine for benefits and other concerts, sometimes as Pinkwind, and both remained true to their community and cultural roots, refusing the blandishments of commercial TV miming or offers by A&R men to make us more fashionable and palatable to the pop audience.

With the late great Mal Dean, a frequent contributor to *IT* as a cartoonist, I did a Jerry Cornelius strip for Mick which, like much of what Mick himself was doing for the paper, seemed to stand the test of time pretty well.

It seems to me that Mick is one of the few who kept the faith where others have turned their "alternative" pasts into little more than career moves, cashing in on their familiarity with the famous and with famous times.

All this has little to do with the book you have here, I suppose, except that maybe it says a bit about the integrity and determination of its author. While I had known Mick casually for a while in the sixties and early seventies I only really began to admire him after I had seen him conducting his own defence during the *IT*/*Nasty Tales* trial in London, which lasted from 9th to 25th January 1973 at the Old Bailey, perhaps the most famous court in Europe, where all the great criminal trials have been conducted for a couple of centuries.

I dropped into the court a couple of times while the trial was going on and on both occasions was lucky enough to see Mick in action. The trial was a fairly typical of a series in London which began, as I recall, with the infamous *Oz* trial and involved London's Special Branch police raiding various premises to carry away and eventually prosecute publications they deemed "obscene" under the notoriously unjust and poorly-constructed law known as the Obscene Publications Act.

Alerted by a complaint from a citizen which eventually turned up at the office of the Director of Public Prosecutions, police officers had raided the offices of *IT,* searching for material they expected to be indictable under the act. Specifically they found copies of *Nasty Tales,* an underground comic of a kind commonly sold in modern bookstores. The police were not only poorly informed and badly trained, they had no clear idea of what they were looking for. Joy Farren, Mick's wife, had been the only person on the premises when they arrived. She had no interest in the comics, working as she did for *IT.*

Nasty Tales had already sold without complaint in the US and UK, running my favourite strip of all time, The Fabulous Furry Freak Brothers, and work by Crumb and others. Rather than risk being defended by an uninformed QC, Mick had elected to defend himself. To be honest I was a little sceptical of his abilities (as I would have been of my own) and was curious to see how he was holding up. Once I got into the public gallery to observe what was going on, I was amazed at the self-control and logic with which Mick addressed witnesses and the jury and it didn't surprise me when he eventually succeeded in getting a Not Guilty verdict. That case was used as a precedent in other trials until eventually the police stopped trying to silence the underground and the world was made safe for the next phase of revolutionary dandyism in the person of punk, The Sex Pistols and Siouxsie and the Banshees.

While the trial had resulted from the complaints of a Mrs. Wooley, whose boy had bought a copy of the comic, the police had been acting out of clear prejudice against what was known in those days as the "underground," the young radicals who demonstrated against the Vietnam War and called for social change.

New Worlds had similar raids and the police had been clearly disappointed not to find the kind of pictures usually published in pornographic magazines of the day. The last such trials were in Manchester in the mid-1980s when Savoy Publications had appealed against the seizure of back numbers of their *Meng and Ecker* and *Reverbstorm* comics and the banning of David Britton's novel *Lord Horror* (check out the Savoy website). Full details of the background to the *Nasty Tales* trial and the proceedings of the trial itself can be found at www.arsydd.bbinternet.co.uk/nastytalestrial1.html and is well worth checking out, if you get the chance, since the site also gives a good sense of the flavour of those times which were at once more invigorating and more depressing than our own. What you'll also find are Mick's answers to the Old Bailey judge and to the prosecution. They are coherent and they are eloquent. They came over even more impressively in the court, what's more, as I can testify.

Since those days, when he was writing for the underground press, Mick Farren has produced a whole series of novels including *The Quest of the DNA Cowboys*, *Synaptic Manhunt* and *The Neural Atrocity* (known as *The DNA Cowboys Trilogy*), *More Than Mortal*, and *Darklost*, most after he moved to the US in 1979 when he saw the writing on the wall and decided to leave the UK to Mrs. Thatcher's hideous attentions.

Give the Anarchist a Cigarette is Mick's often hilarious autobiography, describing the times we both look back on as some sort of golden age, when it seemed as if it was possible to change the world for the better, when we imagined that a period of social justice and equity lay just around the corner.

That it didn't is a measure of our disappointment. That

Mick hasn't altogether given up hope for the future is proof that some people, no matter what happens to them, just can't manage to get very cynical. This book demonstrates that as well as anything could.

Zones of Chaos is a compendium of inventions, interventions, musings and rock and roll lyrics which display the flavour and the fervour of Mick Farren's ongoing life and times. The book is a display case of his obsessions from demons to dope to the dangers and rewards of remaining alive in an increasingly berserk universe.

> We have taken it to the edge of gravity's defile/We have shot out rainbows with our cannon/We have walked with spurs and hard nails over the curvature of planets/And made our mark on iron mountains/ So tell us quickly great hero and man with no name/ What the fuck are we supposed to do now?
>
> I swear mama/I swear before God/If I get through this/ I'm going to be a better man.
>
> Now I don't envy anyone/It causes bloating/And far too many funerals.
>
> What did I do/To finish up here/As some post-Einstein zombie flying dutchman/In a wormhole that I can't get out of
>
> Life's a bitch and then you're infinite

Mick's work is peppered with references to our common culture, from Coleridge to Tolkien, from Elvis to Ian Dury. His fiction bursts with angry ideas, image following image with blinding ferocity. His lyrics are sardonic literature, tragic and funny. His reminiscences are the story of our times. They are an alternative autobiography to his alternative autobiography.

Story or essay, poem or rock song, they all carry the same fierce engagement which has never left this determinedly self-invented individualist whether arguing his case at the Old Bailey or strutting his stuff at London's Roundhouse.

Mick Farren is an original. Read him and rage. Read him

and laugh. Read him and weep. He still has more energy, more life and more creativity in him than most of those who have come after him. And he's still ahead of his own game. Doing what comes naturally. Cocking a snoot at convention. Telling it like it is. Living in a present made incandescent by his very existence. Setting a very bad example indeed. Offering himself as a sacrifice to the gods and goddesses of experience. Showing just how good it is to be alive.

Enjoy this as much as I did. It will turn to gold in your hands.

Michael Moorcock,
Lost Pines, Texas.
April 2008.

Introduction

COMBAT EVOLVED

I heard the words "combat evolved" used on a video game commercial that was airing on the Sci Fi Channel. The phrase resonated over screen images of humanoid aliens in spiky, color-coded armor beating the crap out of mankind who were, according to the voice-over, "outnumbered and outgunned." My first realization was that, right then and there, in this brave new 2009, I felt a bit combat evolved myself, not to mention outnumbered and outgunned.

The idea that writer or poet functions in idyllic conditions of peace and quiet is one of those fond fallacies, fostered by the fans of Emily Dickinson, and those who like to imagine all writers are like poor Franz Kafka, transcribing his paranoid TB horror of the state machine and the potential of insects by the light of a 40 watt bulb, after a hard day clerking. The requirement of peace is also a confidence trick perpetrated by college professors, who only publish once in a decade, and use the idea of seclusion as a cover under which to nap and drink claret. Jack Nicholson's character in *The Shining* also demanded peace and quiet, but he was not doing any writing at the time unless you count "All work and no play makes Jack a dull boy" repeated a few thousand times. He was actually allowing himself to be possessed by the evil forces of the Overlook Hotel, and he was a work of fiction anyway.

Prompted by my own experience, I have to conclude that the writer more normally functions against the short-attention-span audio intrusion of babbling, ground-clutter relayed by a perpetual television, the sirens of emergency service units, the clatter of police helicopters, Howard Stern on the radio, domestic disputes, or Soviet disco in the next apartment, the rasping hornet, two-stroke drone of leaf-blowers, the occasional gunshot, a meteorological back-projection of weather patterns increasingly bent out of shape by the greenhouse effect, and dire news of other mortal threats to the planet.

The external world electronically intrudes with cryptic emails, invitations to pornographic interface, or to sign on for implausible credit cards. The ringing of the phone is ignorable but less so. Caller ID currently sheep-&-goats the corporate demands for money from the friends to whom I want to talk, but the feeling still comes over me that I have been living on borrowed time for at least the last twenty years. Yet then I grin, because, now it's a matter of decades, I may never be asked to pay it back before I die.

I can also tell myself that the now is by no means as hectic as the back-in-the-day when my home was full of dope fiends, speed-freaks, motorcyclists, former White Panthers, future public enemies, and mendicant bloody musicians helping themselves unasked to sandwiches and beer from my refrigeration, and wanting me to write them some sci fi-weight metal lyrics because they were three tunes short of an album. Thus the chance to flee to a secret place that contained nothing more noisy, distracting or needful of attention than the roiling slimy tentacles of Venusian Agents of Galactic Morality was comforting and habitual.

So habitual in fact that very little has really changed. The condition of literary firefight is maintained and the creative imperative lurches through pockets of imagination like a desperate grunt crouching from foxhole to foxhole, or resting up in a shell crater between bombardments. These pockets of imagination are what constitute the Zones of Chaos that provide the title for this collection. At one and the same time they are the refuge of unreality, and the flame-vents of Mt. Doom in which the craft was honed that is now laid out before you, along with some explanation of the process of honing.

The majority of the material in this collection was written in New York and Los Angeles over the last fifteen or so years. I have already described and quoted much of what went before that in my memoir *Give The Anarchist A Cigarette*, and, in the case of the poetry, the best of what survived the 1960s and 1970s were the rock lyrics that are adequately now preserved on CD, and don't commit that well to print. Many of the short pieces in this collection grew into bigger things. Some contributed to novels now published and other are rehearsals for books yet to come. Still more remained exactly as you read them, complete, functional, and at ease with their oneness. Which is a great deal more than can be said for their author.

Mick Farren,
Los Angeles, 2009.

Opening Postures

Shall we begin with the very entities who have made so much of this kind of thing possible? The concept of a demon is a poetic conceit, an attempt to deny that all this driven outpouring is nothing but a product of self-created mania. As the paranoid seeks the comfort of a conspiracy, the poet looks to hardwire himself into a cosmic plan of gods and monsters that he neither fully grasps nor understands, but helps to romanticize the obsession. We all need to put a face to that which drives us. Maybe Stephen King did it best in his novel *Misery*, when he envisioned the motivation to write as a homicidal and psychotic nurse wielding a hammer.

A LONG WALK WITH THE DEMON

All his life he'd walked with the demon
From the Radium Room to the Palace of Mirrors
From the Canadian border to the Place of Skulls
All his life he'd walked with the demon
At regular intervals, his friends had come to him
And pleaded that he cast it from him

The demon drove him to the madness
The craving for the adoration of the mob
The reason that all but one of his women had left him
The demon might mature and modify

Making him more comfortable with the passage of the
     nightmare
But he would never be free

The demon would never let him be free
Never allow itself to be cast out or put aside
Symbiosis, home boy, it told him
A twin singularity

*Written 1993. Recorded the same year with Tijuana Bible
for the CD* Gringo Madness, *released by Big Beat, London
1993.*

The poet complains and complains and complains
some more, but so obviously loves every minute of it.
And when he's not complaining he takes time out to
wonder how the madness should continue, proving
categorically that he has no real plans to arrest the
process, or give up the zones of chaos, no matter
how he might protest.

SONG OF THE HIRED GUNS

We have taken it to the edge of gravity's defile
We have shot out rainbows with our cannon
We have walked with spurs and hard nails over the curvature
     of planets
And made our mark on iron mountains
So tell us quickly great hero and man with no name
What the fuck are we supposed to do now?

We have matched potcheen and double shots of railroad
     gin
With Nazgul of the Ninth International.
And taken abuse to the upper echelons of naked art

We have been and seen and spurned the design,
Abandoned the plan and rejected the plea bargain
So do not leave us hanging
Here in the discolored darkness, Don Vito
For are we not your chosen men?
What the fuck are we supposed to do now?

From sewer and cesspool, trailer park and half crown knocking shop
Feral and fastidious with only a bottle of pills between us
Sharp swords and a fistful of dynamite; songs of victory and execution
We have done the bidding of all and the will of none
We have sacked and pillaged in the cities of the ravaged night
But never except idly and temporarily profited
And it's the time to clue us in, Divine Marquis
For we need to know
What the fuck are we supposed to do now?

Written 2000. Performed live on many occasions, orchestrated by Andy Colquhoun, and recorded for the Deviants' CD, Dr Crow, released by Track Records, September 2002.

Aside from questioning what might happen next and the possible nature of his future function, the poet also ponders what might be his ultimate fate. Here he dons the mantle of the geezer in the barroom, obnoxious, importunate, demanding, and drunk, determined to tell the burdensome story of who he has been and what he has seen, like Coleridge's Ancient Mariner at the wedding. In this piece, the geezer doesn't name himself, but he could easily be a character called Yancey Slide, a demon with whom I've been playing since the late 1980s and who first appeared in my novel *Necrom*.

JUST A POOR DOGPOET WHO FINDS HIMSELF
LOCKED OUT OF THE CATHOUSE

Put a twenty on the bar, my friend
And don't be overly concerning yourself
About receiving any change
Because I will tell you stories
Of bafflement and disbelief
I will weave you webs to amaze and astonish
I will tell you tales of sound and of fury
Signifying...signifying whatever good goddamn thing
You want it to signify
For that is always the choice of those who listen
For that is always the privilege of the crowd
For that is always the deal and the door prize
The dime is under your ownership
You have it your way
That is the rule
Because I am just a poor dogpoet
Who finds himself locked out of the cathouse

Put a twenty on the bar there, pal
And don't look too hard at the stains
On the bartender's apron
The women are ugly, even away from the lights
Unkempt by hard times and harder attitudes
And the air wafts urinal
Under the circling fan
And nobody drinks with Rick
But me, I'm different, my friend
I will drink with anyone
Because I have seen black helicopters over white sand
Running low and mean in Mojave darkness
With galaxies blazing overhead
On dark errands for their unblinking masters
Paid in laser gems and opium

And the attentions of scarlet starlets
But in the caverns they are intolerant of failure
And thus you discover me, pilgrim
Just a poor dogpoet
Who finds himself locked out of the cathouse

Put a twenty on the bar there, stranger
Let the paper marinate in the rings of spillage
While I tell you about how I ran
With the Hashasheens of the New Order
About how we put the fix in on the Chairman
And all but dimmed the lights on the Don
When the guinea gained too great a grasp
Of what was really real
But that was nothing compared
To what we did with the Antichrist
Nostradamus's blue boy in the turban
That long prophesied cocksucker
Really got to suffer
We stuck it to him hard
Cut out his heart and replaced it with a stone
Engraved with the inscription
"Fuck you and the millennium that brought you"
That was the way of it when Hassan IX
Went looking for his righteous vengeance
Unfortunately
His memory was less comprehensive
When it came to the matter of reward
And that is why you now discover me
Just a poor dogpoet
Who finds himself locked out of the cathouse

Put a twenty on the bar there, amigo
And reflect on the highly fleeting nature
Of reward and recompense
And how what truly survives is just a matter of memory
Of perfumed hot sheet nights
Being served by the Elevated of the Pentecost

And each one a true mistress of her Tantric trade
Adept to the eighteenth house
With the accumulated skills and the carnal knowledge
Of fifteen slow centuries of sensual momentum
But coupled with the worldly awareness
That it's always a good idea
To leave with every last pennyweight
Of gold they could get their hands on
So believe me when I tell, seeker after truth
That it can be an effort to accept
The harsh reality
Of a poor dogpoet
Who finds himself locked out of the cathouse

Written 1996. Recorded the same year with Andy Colquhoun and Phil Taylor for the CD Fragments of Broken Probes, *released 1996 by Capt. Trips Records, Tokyo.*

Nostalgia is a close relative of complaint, just as the wistful old-timer recalling his lost loves, the money spent and the stimulants consumed, is nothing but the flipside of the pestering drunk with a tale to tell.

WHEN THE WORLD WAS YOUNG

Back when the world was young
Drunk on cheap well whiskey
And confused on mescaline
Walking rattlesnake curves
On sidewalks that refused to lay down
Resisting
Resisting
Resisting all the importunate invasions of reality

Back when the world was young
Searching for the gateway
To the Secret Garden
The Maps to the Labyrinth
And the Silver Key
With a woman in red shoes
Whose name was maybe Dolores
Dolores?
Or perhaps her name was...Laverne?

Back when the world was young
And fear was so perfectly academic
And the scales were so perfectly poised
That I could still pace the razor's edge
Without cutting my feet or losing any further toes
And I believed
And I believed
And I believed in every fucking drop of rain that fell

Back when the world was young
And you had but to softly ask
The crushed whisper of velvet
The sheer innocence of pure desire
And the requested favor was granted and gratified
So will somebody give?
So will somebody give?
So will somebody please
Give the anarchist a cigarette?

Written 1994. Recorded 1995 with Jack Lancaster for the CD The Deathray Tapes, *released 1995 by Alive Records, Los Angeles.*

But, even for a self-declared anarchist, poetry may grow from strange antecedents...

PYRO WHEN TECHNICAL

As a small boy I'd been both a pyromaniac and a very capable bombmaker. It started at around eight with blowing up my model planes when they would no longer fly, but by age eleven, my friend Adrian Donovan and I were the best junior explosives demolition team in the neighborhood, highly adept at taking out municipal lampposts and the scaffolding on building sites. We had even managed to burn a large hole in a Donovan family carpet while attempting to make nitroglycerine with the equipment from a juiced-up chemistry set. We had followed the outlaw recipe pretty much to the letter, but had completely failed to realize the amount of heat generated by such a reaction. It was enough to melt our test tube very quickly, and dump the smoking and corrosive contents onto the floor of Adrian's bedroom, which it attacked like the acid blood of a Kurt Geiger alien, an occurrence that took a great deal of explaining to Adrian's mum. The odd thing was that I completely gave up my adventures in chemistry with the onset of puberty, except, of course, for those related to chemical ingestion.

A fragment cut and excluded from the finished version of the memoir "Give The Anarchist A Cigarette" published by Jonathan Cape (UK) 2001.

And of what is a poet if he can't find himself thrown in jail now and again? But how many times during an earthquake? No matter how Californians agonize over the Big One, epic seismic events always take us by surprise.

JAILHOUSE ROCK

When the notorious Northridge quake hit the time was exactly 4:31 AM. I'd drifted off to sleep listening to gangsta gossip between Nelson and Conroy in the next bunk. The next moment, the Van Nuys jail was being hammered by a giant baseball bat. One sound and one thought would stay with me forever. The sound was that of every steel door in the joint slamming against its locks and hinges. The thought was "Jesus Christ, it's the big one and I'm locked up in this stinking jail!"

The cage was maybe thirty feet by fifty feet, dimly lit in contrast to the leprously raw neon of the booking area. How I managed to find myself there was hardly relevant. In a minor showdown with the Los Angeles Police Department, they, as in 99% of all the cases, held all the cards, not to mention the guns, clubs, mace and Tasers. Their ace in the hole was that, if they didn't like my attitude, they could toss me in the lockup for 72 hours and ask questions later. In the first moments as I walked in, carrying the blanket I'd been handed, plus the copy of my booking sheet, a comb, toothbrush and miniature tube of toothpaste—the kind you find in the seat pocket on some airlines—I was half blind in the gloom. All I could see were twin rows of narrow, double tier, steel bunks and a crush of dark shirtless figures in baggy boxer shorts. Here it was. The worst nightmare: all the Shawshank cliches of gang rape and sharpened dinnerware. My only protection was a furious adrenaline rush. I was mad as hell and hoping it would be enough to carry me through. No victim attitude.

A steel picnic table stood between the two rows of bunks. With everyone in the room apparently eyeballing the new meat, I furiously hurled down my jacket and blanket. Later, names and personalities will go with the eyes, but right at that moment, I was concentrating on coming through unscathed and I felt indignant rage was my best way to play it. For added fuel, I focused on that my cat Newton has been left without food. Bastard pigs. The other guys were an inverse demographic of the city of Los Angeles. Twenty-four bodies were crammed into the cage, and only two others were white—a long-haired stoner and a hippie curled into a fetal position on the floor. I later learned that the hippie was detoxing from a major heroin habit, with only a handful of Tylenol to see him through. Such is the philosophy of jailhouse drug treatment. "If he don't die, he'll be okay."

By far the largest and most cohesive group were Mexican. Of the fourteen *cholos*, most belonged to a crack-selling street crew, pulled in during a routine Friday night drug sweep. They, and particularly their leader, a muscular, bullet-headed, and highly organized kid called Gomez, turned out to be virtually running the felony tank. Five outnumbered black men, withdrawn and watchful, held their territory on adjoining bunks in a microcosm of L.A. street life, where traditionally black neighborhoods are being squeezed by a constantly expanding Latino-Catholic population. Across the corridor, a dozen or so Aryan Brotherhood tattooed trash were segregated in a separate cage. If these were my ethnic kin, I was happy to be hanging with the homies and the *vatos*.

With the exception of one middle-aged wino, I was a good fifteen to twenty years older than everyone else in the place. Give or take a couple of years, I'm the Keith Richards generation, supposedly old enough to know better and well out of jailhouse practice. My first problem was that I was the last man in and the one remaining bunk lacked its mattress. I noticed that Gomez had an extra mattress rolled up as a pillow. Confrontation or hard metal. Fortunately a third option, basic incarcerate entrepreneurship, came in the form of Hector, Gomez's burly sidekick/lieutenant/bodyguard "Hey, yo, you wanna buy a mattress for a buck?"

Nelson was one of the black minority, coolly immaculate with a clean-shaved head, watching from an upper bunk. "Give him the fucking mattress."

"He shouldn't have come late."

"Next time, I'll try and get busted earlier."

Hector looked at me curiously. "You talk funny."

"That's because I'm English."

"You mean from London? Like the Beatles?"

From that moment on, I answered to "Yo, London." I kept thinking of that old Arthur Lee line. "When I was in England town…" Everyone seemed to assume that I had an encyclopedic knowledge of all things foreign. "Yo, London, is it true that drugs are legal over there?"

"No, but they're less hysterical about them."

The subject of drug legalization did nothing for Nelson. "Legal drugs would just mean more money for the white man."

Everyone in the cage except me and the wino were in on some drug-related beef, but just because we were locked up, it in no way meant transaction or consumption came to a stop. At worst, it was a little more covert and required an advanced degree of ingenuity. But all that was in the future. I still had to get through my own private initiation.

"Yo, London. You got any money."

I was sitting at the picnic table fuming, but rapidly defumed because I recognized this as a moment of truth, and I fucking hate moments of truth. Gomez and five of his crew were gathered round me. Gomez was sitting on one side and Hector on the other, sitting close. Okay, I'll cop to it. I was scared. My flesh crawled in anticipation that something sharp might penetrate it at any second. "It's the way things work, man. Whites hang with us against the niggers."

The moment of truth was in quantum expansion. Draw the line or live with yourself. The word had been dropped like a challenge and I was well aware of Nelson's curious eyes on my back. I'm no fucking hero, but…

"I don't do that."

And nothing happened. Gomez was revealed as more of a pragmatist than I suspected. The challenge had been issued but, not taken, it was left to lie. Gomez had a singular focus on his agenda at hand. "Give us five bucks and we'll be looking out for you."

I'd already made my stand and all things are relative. No macho issue over a lousy five, so I fork it over. The deputies had left me ten in my pocket. Regulations. Six gone and four to go. Just as long as I have enough for a pack of cigarettes when I eventually get out. In the next few hours, though, I learned that Gomez and his crew honored a deal. This weirdass whiteboy is cut in on every piece of contraband they organize.

Bowel movements play a major part in the organization of contraband. Hardly genteel but practical, except maybe for the unfortunate fuck in County who was rumored to have been gutted for the heroin he'd ingested. A primary irony is that, since smoking was banned in California prisons, drugs are the coin of the realm and the traditional tobacco has become a big ticket luxury. Since it's hard to shit cigarettes that are still smokable, a lone Marlboro goes for up to ten bucks.

Hector is curious. "Yo, London, is it true Keith Richards do so much dope he get his blood changed every year?"

"That used to be the story."

"So what happens when they take out all the old blood and before they put the new blood in? Why don't he die?"

Gomez shakes his head. "You one dumb motherfucker, homes. They take the old blood out one end and put the new blood in the other. At the same time, see?"

Back at the earthquake, when the seismic rock & roll stopped, silence, darkness, and the weird smell of institutional dust prevailed. Then the voices started. In crisis, the cage was suddenly functioning as a collective unit.

"Everyone okay?"

"Anybody hurt?"

"Yo, London, what do you figure that was on the Richters?"

I hazarded a guess. "Maybe six point five, going on seven."

As it turned out, I was right on the money and gained beaucoup status for knowing shit. After a couple of minutes, an emergency generator kicked in, and, with light, the first thing we discovered was the guards had gone. The sons of bitches had chickened and run, leaving us locked down like the inevitable convicts who drowned or burned in those Irwin Allen disaster movies. Crazy schemes began to hatch.

The stoner wanted to use the metal picnic table as a battering ram to freedom. Nelson intervened as the voice of reason. "Motherfuckers are probably waiting outside with shotguns to blow us away as we come running out."

"Earthquake turns into Attica?" Some of the youth have never heard of Attica. Nelson and I fill them in.

In an earthquake, the second shock can be more deadly than the first. Already weakened structures give up the ghost, crushing those who have just ventured back inside. The second shock came a couple of hours later. We were all up on our feet as the cage rolled and plaster cascaded down from the ceiling. I dived for the protection of a lower bunk, pulling Nelson down with me. "Yo, London, you think the building's going to come down?"

I was at a loss. "It depends what's on top of us." Though the induction process, I'd lost all structural orientation. Was the cage in the basement? On the first floor? Nelson echoed my confusion. "The man's right. *Where the fuck are we?*"

I'd later realized part of what got me through was that I was willing to pass on any information I had or could theorize. It seemed to gain me a measure of respect as an elder of our ad hoc tribe. The guards, on the other hand, took a perverse delight in the dissemination of mindfuck disinformation. After the second shock, they had sheepishly returned. One who had exhibited a latent measure of decency put a radio in the corridor so we could hear what was what in the world. In a matter of minutes, a sergeant had ordered it shut off. With phones down, we lived in a helpless labyrinth of lurid rumor. The city was burning and the National Guard was shooting looters. The San Fernando Courthouse, one of our routes to freedom, had collapsed. Question a guard about the condition of your own hood and he'd tell you it was in ruins. They were also spreading the story that under a State of Emergency we could be held indefinitely.

Shouting came from the women's section. "Free Willy! Free Willy! Free Willy!" The men looked at each other. "What the fuck are those crazy bitches doing?" Word would later come down that the women had staged a mini-revolt against a

300-pound matron, a fat kissing cousin of Ilsa She Wolf of the SS, who had, with relish, informed a woman suffering a miscarriage that no medical attention was available.

Also proving unavailable were food and water. The story was that there was none, but, when I was eventually released, I walked past crates of bottled water and cases of microwave food stashed in a corridor. As the shocks diminished, a depressed burnout set in. The amphetamine that had been traded off the white trash in return for *cholo* crack was wearing threadbare and the adrenaline from the quake had dissipated. Resigned depression was setting in and jailhouse bullshit resumed—the boasts, the grandiose schemes, the endless speculation regarding conviction and sentencing. The politicians were playing the three-strikes-and-you're-out game, and for Gomez, it seemed inevitable. "If I can't get out of this shit, I'm going to wind up doing fifteen to life. What you think gonna happen, London? I mean, how many of us can they lock up?"

"Maybe they'll build a wall around the whole fucking inner city."

"Like *Escape From New York*?"

Nelson was also in on the conversation and he stared hard at Gomez. "We're fucking communicating here, man. What happened to the race bullshit?"

Gomez shrugged. This was a crisis. Once over, the lines of conflict would be as solid as ever. As far as he was concerned, that too was inevitable. A while later, as if in confirmation, a new arrival was tossed in with us, a young *cholo* whose first move was to crouch down and start trying to sharpen his toothbrush on the cement floor. He had clearly bought into all the legends of mortal danger. Or maybe he *was* in mortal danger. Perhaps he'd been tossed in with the wrong crew. He didn't fare too well. Some kind of rubberized paint on the floor made it impossible to put a combat point on the toothbrush.

The following afternoon, a squad of detectives showed up. Now they wanted as many of us out of there as possible. I was one of the first to be cut loose. As I grabbed my coat and headed for the door, I got a round of applause and my hand shaken. A lot of them now knew I was a writer. Their voices followed me down the corridor. "Write about us, London. You fucking write about us."

Gomez also had a piece of advice. "Don't get in no more trouble, man. You don't belong in this place."

My tenor-playing homeboy, Jack Lancaster, had driven all the way out to pick me up, and, on the way back into Hollywood, past collapsed buildings and fires still burning, it started to look as though we had it easy in the Van Nuys jail. As Jack turned onto Melrose, we ran into a squad of young, nervous, and heavily armed National Guard, outside Spike Lee's rebel clothing store, protecting boutiques from nonexistent looters. I guess law and order is an elastic business.

Written 1995, published in a slightly different form in the Los Angeles Reader, *as a* Panic In The Year Zero *column.*

Rampage and Drunkenness

I freely confess that I have spent a good deal of my life intoxicated. It is not something of which I am overly proud, but, at the same time, I also do not feel any particular need for shame. Should a defense be required at any time, I can only say that it does give one a variety of very interesting perspectives, and that drink and drugs have, by this late in life, proved beyond question that they are by far the most effective tools for maintaining a permanent and wholly portable zone of personal chaos, and ensuring the writing maintains its perfectly honed edge of driven desperation. Be warned, though, the continuous use of this heavy machinery can take its toll of both the liver and the sanity.

TALES OF BEATNIK GLORY

Mona sought eternal gloom, ached for random insect doom
Transcendental Juliette Greco with Elvis Presley slapback
    echo
The Lady Zorro in disguise with saintly smile and junkie's
    eyes
The gamblers all took Bernie's marker, he kept a shrine to
    Charlie Parker
Spoke French on 52nd Street, gobbled whites and didn't eat
Perverse in tactics to confuse, Clauswitz in Italian shoes

And Lisa rolled a defrocked lama and solidly fucked up her
   karma

Looked for answers on the square, enlightenment and savoir
   faire

Drank Sterno with the bowery crowd who stoned her when
   she got too loud

Rachel picked up cops in bars, handcuffed in the backs of
   cars

Agile in her degradation, intellect above her station

Homogenized each book she read, philosophized while giving
   head

And Rae flew backwards from Van Nuys in yellow cab with
   yellow eyes

Raised Genet to the near sublime, the frontier of art and
   crime

Tied off before the Steel Communion, nodding in unholy
   union

While Marcia lived in black and white in Blake's dark forest of
   the night

A camera where the cool convene, a crowd scene from *Mad*
   magazine

Film speed set on extra hurry, a t-shirt that read "What Me
   Worry?"

*Written 1990. Recorded 1995 with Jack Lancaster for the
CD* The Deathray Tapes, *released 1995 by Alive Records, Los
Angeles.*

"Tales of Beatnik Glory", a title I stole from
Ed Sanders, was performed to be-bop. Cool and
finger popping. Six years later I revisited the same
territory in less retro and more millennial guitar
mode, although the story is more integrated, first
person and shamelessly excessive. In performances
of "Tales Of Beatnik Glory", I learned that there's

nothing a raucous poetry crowd enjoys more than epic tales of brutal and apocalyptic shamelessness. Indeed, the more apocalyptic and shameless the better. Also, being raised on rock & roll, I do like a good rhyme pattern.

ON SUCH A LURID NIGHT

The city air was wafer brittle. Too jagged for the scarcely sane
Avoiding interloper's glances, aware that we'd come back again
The ancient crew now reassembled, hallowed sweat in gaudy light
The odds on mayhem swiftly shortening
In the course of such a lurid night
Sweet Anita tactile armored, Baby Joseph hides a gun
Never seen the fix so angry. Spurred us to the contract run
Through all the waterholes of destiny. Drinks all round, now see us right
Commerce long since ceased to signify
In the course of such a lurid night

Marcia springs a roll of hundreds, all the hustlers' eyes are pinned
Ike just racks 'em, "don't say nothing." Marcia grins and Marcia wins
Queens caressing abject sailors, plan to steal a black and white
Civil law might be suspended
In the course of such a lurid night
Like Johnny told us "ain't no future." Each rotten hour as it comes
Mutinous troopers of the evening, distinguished by their rattling drums
On to conquest, on to glory; Martian, Treen or Selenite
Whatever planet you might come from

In the course of such a lurid night

Seals are ruptured, trumpets sounding, the Beast should show up anytime
Hold my horse, postpone apocalypse. This rapture's getting too divine
I could be drunk, I could be falling, poisoned by a malachite
I could even wrestle scorpions
In the course of such a lurid night
A day of reckoning doubtless waiting, if indeed day ever dawns
Then observe the wretched penitent, speared by dilemma's horns
Hell to pay, if Hell can catch me and I ain't going without a fight
I could scale Gehenna's ramparts
In the course of such a lurid night

Written 1996. Recorded 1996 with deviants xvvi for the CD Eating Jello With A Heated Fork, *released 1996 by Alive Records, Los Angeles.*

And, of course, you can't win 'em all. Some binges have a less fortunate outcome than the instant overthrow of Western Civilization as we know it. On the other side of the coin we find the...

HIPPIE DEATH CULT

Alas — I fear
Through my own stupidity
I have become
A foul and hollow creature of Mordor

I woke in a Beverly Hills mansion
Beside the indoor pool
Face down upon the marble surround
With a blinding headache
And the first thing I discovered
Was that everyone else was dead
Stabbed to death with kitchen knives
Fourteen corpses
Sharing a collective total
Of five hundred and eighty seven
Puncture and slash wounds

And there were things
Scrawled on the walls in blood
Pentacles, swastikas, cabalistic symbols
And the slogan
"EAT PORK, MOTHER, YUM YUM!"

And I have this sick feeling in my gut
That the people responsible
Were the ones I came with
The one who were talking Kali worship
And handing out the black and purple capsules

And now the sirens are coming up the driveway
LAPD black & whites
Rolling to the slayfest of the decade
And I'm in this deep
Like I said,
A foul and hollow creature of Mordor

Maybe I should have considered
Maybe I should have thought it through
A little more thoroughly
Maybe I should have reflected more on the outcome...

Before I agreed to join the Hippie Death Cult

Written 1993. Recorded in the same year with Tijuana Bible for the CD Gringo Madness, *released by Big Beat, London 1993.*

The time inevitably comes when every party has outlived its usefulness, but, having taken on a life of its own and become more than the sum of its revelers, it refuses to give up without a fight. Such is the phase of debauch when evil is wont to penetrate the veil.

BEYOND THE END OF THE ATOMIC BOOGIE HOUR

Like English Danny more than once remarked
The world could grow a little weird
Beyond the end of the Atomic Boogie Hour
Like the ratchet of the universe
Had backed up and slipped a couple of cogs
While the Great Brakeman failed to notice
Engrossed as he was in a dirty book

Like English Danny more than once remarked
Odd stuff really did happen
Beyond the end of the Atomic Boogie Hour
A chill would creep as the theme faded
The drop of a faint fractional degree
But enough to set you signaling
To Tattooed Jenny for another tequila
Just to convince yourself it was but illusion
And no pale horse had somewhere whinnied in its sleep
And then Lefty Frizzel would come on the jukebox
And suddenly all was right with the world
Or was it?

Like English Danny more than once remarked

The wraiths did get to walking
And the strange did come to pass
Beyond the end of the Atomic Boogie Hour
Hadn't that been the time
That Masonic Bob had stabbed High Lee
In the left hand for disparaging his Electroglide
And wasn't it always then
That some vodka drunk fool chose to go home
With a woman other than his own
And even we who had the equilibrium
To avoid falling crazy
Would stare a little harder
Into the back bar mirror, avoiding our own eyes
And the spaces at the edge of light
Where conjurous stick figures beckoned to come join
Their nebulous but awesome games

Like English Danny more than once remarked
It could get downright peculiar
Beyond the end of the Atomic Boogie Hour

Written 1995. Recorded 1995 with Jack Lancaster for the CD The Deathray Tapes, *released 1995 by Alive Records, Los Angeles.*

The final phase of every intoxicant atrocity is, sure as night divides the day, the hangover. I have written a great deal about hangovers. When, for my sins, I joined the rock & roll press corps for a while, I would write concert reviews that gauged the performance by the intensity of the hangover the following morning. How much do I hurt? How much did I enjoy The Clash? The one could only be equated with the other, and the readers seemed to understand where I was coming from.

DIABOLO'S CADILLAC

Room 101 and a ratcage on my face
The pain is close to indescribable
The horror, the horror
Last night I took a ride in Diabolo's Cadillac

Morning is beyond the drapes and demons wrench at my
    eyelids
With steel pliers
Blessed Virgin just show me mercy or give me a Valium
Last night I took a ride in Diabolo's Cadillac

My brain is as dry and shriveled as a motherless sponge
And I dread the ultimate re-entry of the blood
When the torture of the damned will resemble a bright day
    at the beach
Last night I took a ride in Diabolo's Cadillac

Jesus, God, give me a break here will you?
It's only a chemical analogue
For those two old dogs pleasure and retribution
I've heard that twelve steps can lead to salvation
But I also recall that one more
Will take you to the gallows
I don't need a stinking program
Just a remission from guilt
And some show about Hitler on the History Channel
To convince me I am not all bad
While I collect my scattered senses
And regain my grip
On my alleged and wretched humanity
Last night I took a ride in Diabolo's Cadillac.

*Written 2000, performed frequently, set to music by Andy
Colquhoun, and recorded for the Deviants' CD,* Dr Crow,
released by Track Records in September 2002. A Diabolo's

*Cadillac is a Long Island Iced Tea with tequila substituted for
the vodka.*

FOUR PIECES FOR DISTURBED ANIMALS

So why, you ask do I choose to commence a section supposedly dedicated to writings about animals with something composed following the death of my friend, accomplice and co-defendant Edward Barker? He may have drunk himself to death in 1997 but he was also one of the gentlest and most innocent beings who ever walked this Earth, which is possibly why the same Earth proved too much for him. He also had a unique gift, or maybe curse, which enabled him to see the human race as cartoon animals.

ANTHROPOMORPHISM

We came to your perception
(Jolly saucy crew)
As crows in zoot suits
Hippos dressed like Elvis
Anxious giraffes, neurotic ostriches
Hairless men in gross ballet
And felines in pullovers
So short and tight
They couldn't hide the beer gut
But, for chrissakes
Edward, dear boy,
Did we ever ask you
To walk point for this platoon?
Or be the fucking scout
For the final frontier?

Written 1997 on the death of the cartoonist and illustrator, Edward Barker, and read by Felix Dennis as a part of his eulogy. Previously published as part of the funeral service program.

Big dogs played a major part in the survival of my hell-spawned childhood. Later, when I became a city dweller instead of a country boy, I switched my loyalties to felines, and have pretty much had one as a companion ever since. Here, of course, the dog is not a companion but the spectral device to take us to that Robert Johnson world where hellhounds haunt the crossroads, and abandoned mansions loom from the swamp miasma with blind, zombie blank windows. It's a nice place to visit, and I even spent a few months living there.

GHOST OF THE YELLOW DOG

Ghost of the yellow dog been walking
Whispering names and laying on burdens
Making it clear that no more deals
Will be transacted at the midnight crossroads
And there's a train pulling out of St. Petersburg
Time go on, time go on

Ghost of the yellow dog been stalking
Chilling the pulses of clandestine lovers
And securing the bonds of iron and satin
And souring the sweet new wine of passion
And there's a train highballing it
Into the yards by Jacksonville
Time go on, time go on

Ghost of the yellow dog been howling

Calling to others of his ilk and kind
In the mist shroud of the reeds by the alkaline water
Closing the casebook on crimes neither planned nor
    imagined
And there's a train running fast on corroded rails
On the Vicksburg-Danbury spur
Time go on, time go on

Ghost of the yellow dog been prowling
Knowing more than was ever fitting
Even for those in the comfort of the coffin
Hellhound recall of lost grey horsemen
And the creak of saddle leather weary from conflict
And there's a train rattling slats of the old wooden trestle
Out in the distance by the county line
Time go on, time go on

The ghost of the yellow dog been roaming
Quick, close the shutters, extinguish the lamp
Roll a cigarette in wheatstraw paper for High John the
    Conqueror
That train's pulling into the station
Momentarily
Time go on, time go on

*Written 1994. Recorded 1995 with Jack Lancaster and Brad
Dourif for the CD* The Deathray Tapes, *released 1995 by
Alive Records, Los Angeles. Another more blueswailing version
with Andy Colquhoun on solo guitar appeared on the 1998*
The Deviants Have Left The Planet *released by Capt. Trips
Records, Tokyo.*

    In the city of Interzone, the Three Headed Boy
is never king. Indeed, the crustaceans constitute a
decidedly oppressed minority. The Ever Hungry
Bikini Women have retractable claws and perhaps

other feline characteristics.

THREE HEADED LOBSTER BOY

After the morning executions
The Three Headed Lobster Boy
Customized his carapace
A hand rubbed flamejob
Scarlet through canary yellow
On ten coats of midnight metalflake
In the manner of Big Daddy Ed Roth

The Three Headed Lobster Boy
Had hoped that his new paint
Would gain the approval
And win the affections
Of the Ever Hungry Bikini Women
But the Ever Hungry Bikini Women
Merely hissed
Flexing and unsheathing
Their retractable claws
In a singular display of contempt and hostility

We don't like you
Three Headed Lobster Boy
Your antennae are bizarre

Stealthily
In the isolation of red night
The Three Headed Lobster Boy
Would slip the confines of his cone
And vacate the silence
Entering the sector of the vertebrates
Following the conduits and the moisture lanes
Drawn by the blue electricity
That darted on the deserted patio
Outside of Sophia's Cabaret

From where he could watch
Unobserved
As, on the inside,
The Ever Hungry Bikini Women
Disported, lewd and serpentine
With troopers of the Secret Legion
And agents from the Office of Public Order

But eventually he would be spotted
Betrayed by his florid excitation
And then he would become
The target of the wrath of the Ever Hungry Bikini Women
Who would pause in their wanton encirclement
Hissing again with cruel perception

Go away Three Headed Lobster Boy
You can offer us nothing
That could be considered to our advantage

And to contain his misery
The Three Headed Lobster Boy
Would ingest complex fluorocarbons
Through the soft flesh
Beneath the junctions in chitin plates

And when discovered
Prone and insensate
And ejected from the sector
By the Civil Guards
The Ever Hungry Bikini Women
Would laugh their laugh
And nod knowingly

We will never encircle you
Three Headed Lobster Boy
Because we are humorless
And you have no spine

Written 1995, recorded 1996 with Deviants xvvi for the CD Eating Jello With A Heated Fork, *released 1996 by Alive Records, Los Angeles.*

Now that humanity has started to behave like a virus, it becomes increasingly hard for many to accept they ain't nothing but a higher primate. I know it was Agent Smith in *The Matrix* who accused mankind of being a virus, but the facts are pretty much borne out by computer models. Computers do, of course, have a very dim view of us. Both *The Matrix* and *2001: A Space Odyssey*, make that abundantly clear. In this observation I adopt the alien opinion that we need to remember we are only smart monkeys who happened to stand up for long enough to see over the long grass, and almost immediately grew too big for our evolution.

BIG TROUBLE ON THE MONKEY PLANET

The last time that I was abducted by aliens, I returned with the distinct impression that they were close to the end of their extra-terrestrial rope with the Third Stone from the Sun and, in particular, its overdeveloped, tool-using, simian inhabitants. Namely us, the human race. When one of those lipless little grey suckers with the bald heads and huge guppy eyes came up to me, right there in the main abductee reception area, a charmless place not unlike Ontario airport with an added dimension, and wanted to know "when the hell are you Earth monkeys going to stop breeding yourselves into extinction," I had to accept the fact that we may not be the most admired life form in this neck of the quadrant.

I rarely admit my abduction experiences. Not so much because I'm embarrassed by them. It's more that I've never really felt that my encounters had been significantly productive. I tended to talk about them rather more when I lived in New York. I discovered that, on 14th Street, if you told the guy on the next bar stool that you were an UFO abductee, he would more than likely dismiss you as crazy, but mercifully harmless. Try the same thing at a party in Venice and they'll not only totally believe you but proceed to recount their own adventures in space, usually centering on intrusive alien surgical procedures, often of a gynecological nature. Some will even give you the number of a therapeutic support group.

It was during the initial medical examination that the ETs started to discover that I was hardly the experimental subject of their collective dreams. I was first abducted at a time when I was drinking even more heavily than usual. It solved the missing time problem, but my blood alcohol level spiked out and created chaos butterflies in their nano-stats. Even worse, my chromosomes had been so customized by the quantities of LSD 25 that I'd consumed during an earlier bout of destructive self-exploration, that I was pretty much useless as a source of genetic material, unless, of course, someone or something wanted to breed a race of nappy-haired tadpoles with nasty imaginations. Rumors also circulated that, when particularly fucked up, I would show a less than appropriate affection for the rectal probe.

In terms of the normal conventions of Earth/alien interaction, I pretty much proved myself a social incompetent, and I would never have been abducted again had the implant not already been in the small of my back, just to the left of my spine. This means I'm solidly on the tracking computer, and can be hauled up for a bogus 20-thousand-light-year service at anytime, and there isn't a damn thing that I or any other bio-entity can do about it. I don't want to see them, they don't want to see me, but, like junk mail and unwanted relatives, they just keep coming around.

This was surely the reason that, after the third routine beam up, I was shuffled aside to hold gentlemanly if sometimes oblique conversations with Qua/D/Thrrof, the discursive focus of a being, essentially a form of highly intelligent yeast, about nine thousand miles long and one molecule thick, that makes its home in a loose orbit around Jupiter. Qua/D/Thrrof was the first alien to make crystal clear what I'd already suspected. As far as the rest of the inhabitants of the viable cluster are concerned, here on the Monkey Planet (as Earth is commonly known), we are in big trouble. That's why, even after twenty thousand years, we still haven't emerged from the quarantine phase as laid down in the Prime Directive. (He also confirmed how Tom Tomorrow's theory about the Republican Party and Rush Limbaugh being a secret alien test of human stupidity is uncannily on the money.)

Like most foreigners, Qua/D/Thrrof blames a considerable proportion of Monkey Planet woes on the affluent of the United States. (Or, as they call them, The Resource Gobblers.) In our most recent conversation, he expressed trepidation over how 2000 AD is a Presidential election year, and the escalating horror of the phenomenon might, this time round, actually push us over into a collective, species-wide, greed-barking psychosis.

"I don't know why you don't just get rid of democracy." Qua/D/Thrrof has a certain problem grasping concepts like the rights of the individual, coming as he does from a collective consciousness of over two billion component facets. He's good, however, at accepting nuances like how election finance reform is fundamentally impossible because the television stations end up with the lion's share of the bucks, and around election time, politics yields more ad revenue than headache remedies, phone sex and psychic hotlines combined.

"Just get rid of television." Even other passing aliens realized that Qua/D/Thrrof was elaborately out of touch with this remark. A small green person with tentacles and huge ears sadly shook what approximated for a head. "It's only television that keeps them from killing each other more than they already do. If television hadn't been introduced in the fifties, they'd be into mechanized erotic cannibalism by now. You know what the monkeys are like when you leave them to their own devices."

Another received snippet of intergalactic gossip is that our Earth, despite its quarantine, is getting the reputation as a clandestine hangout of vermin and lowlife. High on the list are the crew of retard hot rodders and nova scum from Zeta Reticuli who've been putting on the lightshows out at Area 51, just north of Las Vegas, and sending the conspiracy paranoids into uproar. It would seem that these alien Hells Angels have managed to convince the U.S. military that they are the Supreme Authority in the Universe, rather than the malicious honky tonk sweepings of a hundred parsecs, and now have total run of the Pentagon.

What really worries Qua/D/Thrrof, however, is our galloping overpopulation. "Surest way to foul up a perfectly good planet. You either got to stop breeding or start dying." Qua/D/Thrrof is especially pissed at the Catholic Church and their attitudes on population control. As he puts it, "Jesus was one of ours in the first place. It's kinda embarrassing."

Another serious consideration would seem to be that many aliens feel that our Earthling stupidity is playing directly into the hands of some galactic political hard liners. Apparently the stampede to the bellicose right is not confined to only this solar system. An entire multi-species mindset would be just as happy to fire up the Great Planet Fryer and turn this whole messy sphere that we call home into one vast, fused, green glass Christmas tree ornament. Seemingly they view Earth as something akin to a planetary welfare case.

Like they say on the *X-Files,* "The truth is out there." Or at least some approximation of it.

Written 1996. First published 1996 in The Los Angeles Reader *as a column in the* Panic In The Year Zero *series.*

Contortions of Passion

To quote from memory, Che Guevara once pointed out that "At fear of seeming ridiculous, no revolution can succeed unless founded in love," but love has become a word which is used to cover a true multitude of sins and a million unchained melodies. Love Hurts, Love Is Strange, Love Stinks, Love Is A Many-Splendored Thing, Love means never having to say you're sorry, All You Need Is Love, Love Me Do, Love Me Tender, It's A Thin Line Between Love and Hate, Baby Love, Who Do You Love?, A Love Supreme, a Love that dare not speak its name, Love On The Rocks, Love On The Dole, Love's Labors Lost, Stop In The Name Of Love, I Love New York, I Love Bumblebee, Bumblebee tuna. Or as Elvis sang with profound insight, "Treat me like a fool, treat me mean and cruel, but love me."

ANY QUESTIONS?

The world is controlled
By a giant computer and seven women
The computer is set in ferro-concrete
Two hundred feet below Babylon
But the women can never be located
Particularly when you want them
Any questions?

Written 2000, never previously published except as a web post.

The short pornographic sketch that follows was totally inspired by the Tijuana Bibles, the dirty little 1930s, Depression-era sex comics for which our musical combo was named, and movies like Martin Scorsese's *Boxcar Bertha*. In a Jim Thompson motel room, the low oxygen, valve-radio malaise of sex, unfiltered cigarettes, suspenders, and cheap bourbon of a brand you don't recognize is damned to eternity.

WHILE THE OTHER ONE WATCHED.

The shorter one in the striped shirt and black socks fucked her while the taller one in the two-tone wingtip shoes and suspenders sat in a chair and watched from about three feet away; and it was 1935, and she had no idea how she'd got there. Not that it wasn't listlessly enjoyable in a sleazy, slatternly, and transcendentally sordid way. The flapper dress was pulled up past her waist and the top open so the short one could touch her tits if he took a mind to. Or the tall one could look at them. A pink plush stuffed bear like a prize on the carnival midway lay on the pillow beside her, and she was still wearing her Joan Crawford hat with the net veil.

The short one hadn't bothered to take off her rolled-down stockings or even her panties. He'd just moved them to one side so her cunt was accessible. She softly gasped each time he thrust into her. It wasn't what one might call pleasurable, but it didn't hurt and it was comforting to have a function in the situation. *Lil' Orphan Annie* was playing on the upright radio. "Arf arf, Sandy. Do the dog." Very soon the short one in the striped shirt would probably take it into his head to have her turn over so he could do the dog. She didn't care. It would at least be a change of scenery. Or maybe the tall one would want to take a turn. She didn't care. She suspected that the tall one was content to watch. Or maybe he'd want to tie her up or fuck her in the ass. Still she didn't care. At least he hadn't climbed aboard and wanted her to suck him while the other one went on relentlessly humping. She'd even been ready for that scenario. Maybe later she'd get to watch while they did each other. Fresh boys out of jail were like that.

Every so often, the tall one would pass the short one the mason jar of 'shine and the short one would stop thrusting into her to take a drink. At least he was enough of a gentleman to offer her the jar. "You wanna belt, honey?"

Her response was routine and hardly ladylike. "Of course I want a fucking belt. I wouldn't be fucking doing this if I wasn't fucking drunk."

In fact, she had no idea why she was doing this. Or if indeed any of it was real. She knew in the past there'd been a jailbreak with searchlights and slaughter, a Packard Roadster, a Tommy Gun and automatic pistols. But it wasn't a real memory. Just an unseen preamble. Nothing was truly recalled and nothing truly existed outside of this room. Maybe never did and never would. "You know we're all going to Hell for this?"

The tall one lit one Camel off the last. "We're in Hell already."

That would explain everything.

Written 1999, never previously published.

"Before you light that blasted cigarette could you unlock this expensive and sophisticated device so I can move my damned head?" How far is it from pornography to love behind its masks and cross-references of ownership, sensual exploration and guilt? Will my electricity polarize with your electricity? My sickness match your sickness?

After recording the following piece, I was delighted to learn that one critic likened the delivery to "an evil Jeremy Irons." Actually it was the critic's daughter, but that makes it all a little too complicated for brevity.

THE ARTS OF DARKNESS

When alternative attractions were exhausted
And the other recreations of the evening
Had become colorless and mundane
They retreated to the finality
Of her most closed of chambers
Removed their outward personalities
And practiced the arts of darkness
Although he considered the word practice
Fundamentally redundant
Hadn't each well evolved rite and ritual
Been so precisely and repeatedly performed
Down the intense and Kafka twisting passages of time
That the two of them
Were now movement perfect
In the complex dance scenarios of their vice?

No word
No whisper
The mere sigh of suggestion
And he would
By necessity comply
Infinitely malleable
In the secrecy of their golden silence
And scarcely bearable anticipation
Hearing nothing
But the momentary electric friction
Of silk and languid lace
And a soft snap
And indrawn breath
As deviant devices
Completed their love connection

When his mouth grew too dry

She would pour the wine
Cut crystal and arctic ice
On bruised recipient lips
Small rainbow refractions across contusion
And a momentary reversal of role
As she waited on him like a servant
When the assigned intelligence
Dictated that it was he
Who would wait and serve
And wait again
Never knowing where or when
The next intensity
Would bestow its mark

And when he was not otherwise impaired
Impaled or restrained
He might covertly raise his eyes
To focus on the smaller details
The needle points of light
The cutting edge
Of the profound and the impossible
The intricacy of a costume fastening
Or the exact interface where soft silver
Made its penetration
Or the red orange-dark burning of her cigarette
That inevitably bore the scarlet lipstick traces

When alternative attractions were exhausted
And the other recreations of the evening
Had become colorless and mundane
They rctrcatcd to the finality
Of her most closed of chambers
And practiced the arts of darkness

*Written 1995. Recorded 1996 with deviants xvvi for the
CD* Eating Jello With A Heated Fork, *released 1996 by Alive
Records, Los Angeles.*

Back when I lived in New York City, there was a radio station — KLYT or something — that had the plainly absurd but much touted format of playing "love songs, nothing but love songs." Me? I've never been that big on love songs. I generally leave that kind of thing to Paul McCartney and Barry White, but, now and then, I rise to an occasion as in the time when my long-time girlfriend Susan Slater jetted off to Los Angeles and I foolishly tarried in NYC. Hurting and honest, I penned the following that was orchestrated and beautifully sung by John Collins when it came to digital fruition.

THE SCARS NEVER SHOW

Spider woman, the night I betrayed you
Dark lady, the guilt is there still
For dreams that all died with the fear of destiny
And a fifth of Jack Daniels and too many pills

Scarlett O' Hara, I died at the airport
Blanche Dubois, I drown in the flames
And you're in the Lotus Room, lunch with the Joker
And I'm in the shadow, learning my name

But I've got the grandeur of grand isolation
In the deeps of the city, I know where to go
And I've got protection, TV in the small hours
And my shoulders are hunched so the scars never show

Vampire princess, no light in the mirror
Vampire queen, the sun can't get through
Safe in our coffins, secure from reality
But in the dark earth, dreams never come true

But I've got the grandeur of grand isolation
In the deeps of the city, I know where to go
And I've got protection, TV in the small hours
And my collar's turned up so the scars never show

   *Written 1987, recorded by John Collins with Wayne Kramer
on the CD* Deathtongue.

   From Pete Townshend's "La-La-La-Lies" to Lou
Reed's "Femme Fatale" plus a good fifty percent
of the entire work of Bob Dylan, every poet needs
to have created at least one large and overbearingly
misogynist anthem. This is mine. It is not the
product of any specific incident, just the combined
memory of all of those who ever done me wrong,
and, of course, totally ignoring the simple fact
that, at times, truth is the last thing required in a
relationship.

I KNOW WHEN YOU LIE

Abandon the will, release the judgement
The day dwindles
And the process of logic with it
It is pointless to struggle, my proud beauty
Or desire that which is no longer an option
I know when you lie
You lie when you move your lips.

The great river slow surges at its own sweet speed
And sets its own agenda with relentless flow
The high running tide has no consideration
Of the sensuous curvature of time
Other than that which it sets for itself
The ice has long since melted, my dear

The polar caps have gone
Baton Rouge is under water
Galveston is inundated
And even your gin and tonic
Is rapidly nearing room temperature.

Abandon the will, release the judgement
The day dwindles
And the process of logic with it
It is pointless to struggle, my precious temptation
Or desire that which is no longer an option
I know when you lie
You lie when you move your lips.

You in the house
Bring out your greedy dead
Free yourself from the grip of their fingers
You owe them nothing
And they, in turn, have bequeathed you no legacy
Relinquish the memories, oh femme fatale
The tumbrils are waiting
The range of choice has narrowed to the inevitable
In this nuclear winter of our romance.
So believe me that, in a very little while
You will desire nothing more and nothing less than
To smoke one or more of my handmade cigarettes.

Abandon the will, release the judgement
The day dwindles
And the process of logic with it
It is pointless to struggle, my recalcitrant love
Or desire that which is no longer an option
I know when you lie
You lie when you move your lips.

Written 1999, never previously published.

HEROES

The purpose of heroes of either gender or none must be to keep our legends alive. The warriors, the philanderers, the artists and revolutionaries, the gilded ghosts who died before both their time and ours, provide the faces for the aspirations of the tribe, or generic names for all of those who have faced the fear in one form or another. Heroes can be the yardstick of our pride and our perversity in almost equal measures.

The challenge of the project that follows was to produce a piece of art that was reflective of any song by Jimi Hendrix. As a product of the multimedia sixties I would obviously have preferred to write an actual video game, but I am far too old and lacking in the expertise to even approach such a thing. Thus I wrote a short story about a video game. I was also provided with a chance to exercise my voodoo chops that I would use more fully in the novel *Jim Morrison's Adventures in the Afterlife*.

THE VOODOO CHILE EXPERIENCE

The otaku panic took hold of Zeno from the very moment that the door of his room closed behind him. He had a lot of trouble with the outside world. Had the word not hit the spam that the Fat Greek was selling Voodoo Chile, Zeno would never have made such a trip so early in the month. In the outside world, the sky was too vast and the people beneath it were too crowded together, too noisy and too unpredictable. The dirt, and the smell, the cumbersome randomness of external reality rasped on his anxieties. His self-preserving alarms tripped and set his heart to hammering behind a rush of desperate adrenaline. Go back inside, Zeno. You don't like it out here.

Before he could even make it through the street entrance, he had to take three or four deep and deliberate breaths to force back the flutterings. After the deep breathing, he straightened his spine under the anonymous green-drab gas cape. Walk tall, walk straight, without the otaku, shut-in cringe that all too obviously labeled you to the Neanderthals as a no-problem victim. Despite all mental and physical preparations, however, he still had difficulty. From the moment that he set foot on the sidewalk and turned up his collar against prying eyes and the dreary grey drizzle that drifted down ever cyclically on the city, he had to expend a great deal of nervous energy fighting back the desire to cut and run for the safety of his fourmat, his futon and his warm dark bunker of hardware.

It wasn't that Zeno was a coward. No chicken he. In his own reality, he could be both piratical and reckless, and grin like a fool as he diced with disconnection and risked his very sanity among the fractal spikes and trick complexities on the high planes of Tracery Model or Turbo Stormcrow. Wasn't it acknowledged by the others in his pod that he was more than willing to risk suspension and even the unthinkable grounding by thumbing his nose at the Q-Sec monitors as he slipped into a closed room or bypassed a no-go? The gulf between his kind and the rest of the monkey world had simply grown too vast for effortless transition. De-evolution had washed in on the third wave and relegated the outside to television minds and dirty stunted thoughts of fear and carnage.

On the crowded Gilligan's Island of the monkey world, they communicated in grunts and fondled their diseases, and Zeno made as little contact with it or them as he possibly could. He knew, of course, that they were always out there, but, in his fourmat, in one of a million tenement conversions, the law of averages dictated that they would rarely bother him unless he actually went among them. The grocery delivered. The stipend checks and the payments from Sony were directly deposited, and the only menu for out-venture was the replenishment of his cash and the purchase of those items, both legal and proscribed that could not be remote-ordered on the net. In a more normal time, Zeno would not have made such a run out until maybe around the twentieth or twenty-first, but this wasn't a normal time. The Fat Greek was selling Voodoo Chile.

For eighteen months, ever since he'd first heard tell of it, Zeno had waited for a straight shot at Voodoo Chile. No less than three times, he had believed that the elusive program was all but within his grasp. On each occasion, though, the chance had proved to be a near miss, a blind alley or a fiction. The Voodoo Chile software was all but legendary, not only on account of its rarity and the difficulty of its procurement, but also by the extent of its mondo-illegality, an illegality that superseded any Q-Sec beef of suspension and check stoppage. The common holding and simple possession of Voodoo Chile stood to take the entrapped or the guilty into the iron, cage-slam hideousness of Federal Agents, a three ring judicial process that could be likened unto Kafka and a finality of hard jail time. The reason the Feds had their nuts in a knot over Voodoo Chile and other programs of its ilk was painfully simple. Voodoo Chile had the potential of a one-way. Voodoo Chile wasn't nasty-nasty like FEC or Redrage. No sticking and hacking in Voodoo Chile. Oh no. Quite the reverse. Voodoo Chile was, by all reports and rumors, threateningly sublime. When you went into Voodoo Chile you boldly went, in all senses of the old adage, and whether you came back was anyone's guess.

As the Feds told it, Voodoo Chile, in a high sixty-two percent of habituals, happied out the user, reducing him or her to tongue lolling brain damage. They called it user fatal and banned it, as they had banned Chitter and Thjong before it. They went on TV and the cheap end of the net and talked about Voodoo Chile as though it was the cybernetic equivalent of jerking off with your head in a plastic bag. The otaku knew better, of course. Those who refused to exit Voodoo Chile were only destroyed within the limited criteria of the Feds and the monkey world. Not dead but gone discorporate. The so-called brain dead explored, forever and amen, fresh and strange neuron deep netherworlds only hinted at by the existing extreme limits.

The Fat Greek was strictly monkey world from behavior to environment. She dealt illegal software to support a massive Percodan, sucrose and polyglutamate combo-habit and a pretty Eurasian boyfriend whose good looks gave him a close to religious disinclination to gainful enterprise. The first drawback was that the Fat Greek lived way over on the other side of town where the street numbers became letters and humanity ceased to be merely oppressive and turned overtly hostile with the added option of being armed. The journey to the Fat Greek's domicile was the longest piece of traveling by foot and subway that Zeno had done in many a month, and the protracted avoidance of street casual eye contact had all but drained him. The Fat Greek lived in an old-fashioned, unconverted railroad flat in a talk-up, one heater, with ragged epsilon pass-cardies and their unmistakable stench huddled on the landings and in the twists of the stair.

By contemporary standards the Fat Greek's apartment was spacious going on opulent, although it appeared that she rarely, if ever, emerged from the womb cocoon of her emperor-sized bed. The debris in the place was monumental and the squalor a matter of dedication. She received Zeno with no attempt at ceremony or even courtesy. Bleary on pillows, with the Eurasian asleep beside her, she was garbed in a black Victoria's Secret peignoir that revealed far more than Zeno cared to grok of her over ample, pink-white, cellulite mountain flesh and the Glock in the shoulder holster worn next to the selfsame skin.

The retail class, the Fat Greek and her kind, were the ones who took the brunt of the Federal heat. The sellers rather than the buyer-habituals, unless they were exceptionally careless, suffered the raids, arrests and incarcerations. In addition, the retailers frequently had no clue as to the awesome truth of their merchandise. Like this organic-indulgent, lard-pile of woman in the vast bed, they were obese immobiles, skinny tweakers or narcoleptic junkies, who favored chemicals over connection, and were only drawn down to trade the black software by the quantum profits generated by their merch's very illegality.

The conversation was minimal. A parade of otaku whispered through her apartment at all hours of the day and night, and the Fat Greek knew the pointlessness of small talk. Zeno removed the brown bag of cash from the zippered inner pocket of his green-drab and laid the soft, threadbare pile of old bills on the counterpane of her bed like a sacrificial tribute. In her turn, she took a plastic bag containing the card and a spare conversion gate from some mysterious orifice in the depths of the bed. With the transaction transacted, all that remained was the wrack of the journey home, again avoiding the eyes of the monkey world, but this time also radar tense for the echo of a Fed footfall and the authoritarian death grip. The possibility always existed that the Fat Greek was being watched.

Regaining once more the familiar security of his fourmat, Zeno was gripped by a transcendental excitement. Having shucked off his green drab boots and bulky street clothing, he almost reverently removed the gate and the card from the plastic bag. For a full ten minutes, he did nothing but squat in his underwear and stare at the two items, relishing the prospect and promise of that which was to come, and declining even to entertain the paranoia that the card might not contain Voodoo Chilc at all, but merely some junk bogus program that the Fat Greek had employed to rob him. That he could be ripped in this way was all but unthinkable. He doubted that his karma could be in such negative balance and the Fat Greek, although unsavory in person, had a reputation to maintain that she would hardly jeopardize by working a cheap switch. Unless, of course, the jones had pushed to some short-term wickedness of deception. With addicts, that eventuality could always cloud a transaction.

Zeno was aware that, to some extent, he was avoiding the moment of truth. The proof was in the perception and he had to proceed to perceive. His movements were almost casual as he snapped the Voodoo Chile card into an external port of the old and heavily customized NK Alpha that served him as a master controller. He waited while it loaded. Outwardly he showed no more emotion than if he'd been routinely laundry listing. His movements were swift, precise, revealing nothing of his conflicted inner turmoil. Finally, the primary screen cleared and the equivalent of a copyright box appeared.

THIS PROGRAM IS A FULL SENSORY CREATION OF THE BLACK AVENGER. BEHOLD YOU MORTALS AND TREMBLE.

Zeno understood that Black Avenger boasted not idly. Legend-word was that it had been he, back in his wild days, who had shit-canned the entire air traffic control at Templehof, and taken the karma for the resultant airwreck passenger massacre. This notice remained for some ten seconds and them was replaced by a second.

THIS PROGRAM IS BASED ON THE MUSICAL WORK VOODOO CHILE BY JIMI HENDRIX RENDERED TO A TOTAL SENSORY EXPERIENCE BY THE BLACK AVENGER. (BEHOLD YOU MORTALS etc.)

The second was replaced by a third. This time, it was a quasi-copyright warning. Most black programs were preceded by a disclaimer of this kind.

USE OF THIS PROGRAM HAS BEEN DEEMED ILLEGAL UNDER THE FULL SANCTION OF FEDERAL AND LOCAL LAW. AS SUCH, IT IS NOT PROTECTED BY CONVENTIONAL COPYRIGHT PROTOCOLS, BUT UNAUTHORIZED COPYING AND MISUSE CAN RESULT IN SUDDEN AND VIOLENT RETRIBUTION.

The warning then gave way to just three words.

POWER MADE ABSOLUTE.

The three words flashed three times and then faded. A new window appeared.

CONNECT RECEIVERS NOW.

The instruction was redundant. The Packard Bell exosuit that was Zeno's main receiver always remained connected. When he wasn't actually experiencing it, it sat hunched on its stand like a dark blue, inert crustacean, silent, but online and ready. Dressing in the suit was one of Zeno's few true tactile contacts that he wholly relished. He drew on the torso unit, the legs and sleeves, the gloves and finally bowed his head to the crowning disorientation of the first few moments in the helmet as the real retreated and the virtual became his all. Initially, he had the tunnel effect, but then his senses settled and the falling sensation left him along with the easy concepts of up, down and depth. He drifted in a ready room, in a magnet breeze of proto-color and shoals of random, spiraling pixels.

FLEX RIGHT GLOVE TO PROCEED. (Yes) No.

Zeno's right hand snapped to a fist, and all was made black in the first impenetrable absence. The final tease of anticipation and the ever present startup uncertainty that nothing would happen and he would remain to eternity, starvation or death, windwalking in nothingness. And then tiny flecks of light rushing at him from a great silent distance. The light came as heralds to the sound, drawing up from the silence, the first rustling wah-wah chicken pecks rising in volume and then the solo Jimi primal theme, closing around his inertia and guiding him forward through the entry system, drifting him surely through apertures in great floating ideograms of polished steel, that exhorted him to pay attention, as they rose over the infinite curved parallels of the virtual horizon like huge irregular and vertical airships, unreadable but known and certain, obvious in their courses and meanings. (Damn, but the Black Avenger was. Good. Brilliant. Awesome.) The theme repeated, liquid blue splashes of high hat and the blossoming of tentative percussion. A cartoon sign hammered into its own cratered spacerock, much in the manner of when Bugs Bunny had his encounters with the invading Martians, bore the words...

"WAIT FOR IT, SCHMUCK!"

The full bore power hit like a breaking tsunami. Even expected, it came as a shock of joy and Zeno was spin curled and hurled — although precious little of his Zeno identity was happening at that point — to drown or ride the wave. For an instant he caught a culture back blossom, a flash from the time of Hendrix. Zeno was the chromium man hanging chromium ten on the chromium board, and the vision stabilized his forward motion. But Silver Surfing was too crude for anything but instantaneous ajustment in a Black Avenger creation. Literacy split and he was an electron entity, slipsliding and pinballing the magnetic field of a Stratocaster as big as a galaxy, micro through macro, and Marshall stacks like the monoliths of distant watching guardians. The bass line pulsed beneath him, a dark double helix boring in to the rock of ages. (While somewhere in a marginal note, Wesley Snipes argued with Woody Harrelson, in the movie *White Men Can't Jump,* that Jimi's rhythm section was never ever white, never in a million years, you dumb ass, hillbilly motherfucker.)

The magnetic fields turned schematic, a switchback grid of undulating blue lines and crackling force plasma that he rail-rode by the dictates of a baroque and capriciously shifting gravity. Robert Johnson, Johnny Shines, Little Richard's Daddy and Maitre Ka-Fu, (the Master of the Crossroads) waited at the initial intersection, at Blue Bayou, offering a jug of white lightning and the option to branch to roots, but Zeno highballed on by. Maybe as a part of some later excursion. In the neophyte time, stay the main course.

WELL I'M STANDING NEXT TO A MOUNTAIN
CHOP IT DOWN WITH THE EDGE OF MY HAND

Tectonic plates shifted uncomfortably and Alps split their fault lines as Atlas shrugged. The tiny women sang and Mothra woke on Monster Island. Boulders big as asteroids cascaded down to geo-apocalypse, now and forever and formative planets gathered debris greedy for the first critical mass. (Damn, but the Black Avenger was. Something.) Boulders rose and fragments reformed, knitting together into cellular coherency. Zeno no longer surfed. He was momentarily adrift upon a summer sea. Lazy lotus islands idled past on siren sighs beneath a purple velvet void. The great flux became a single curving swell and Zeno's entirety was suffused with a golden sun-warmth and all anxiety fell away, but then the light began to fade in a tropical sunset, colored like love's adoring bruise, and an edge of excitement energized him to a new expectancy. Bright letters of fire, jagged as the mark of Zorro, streaked across the now indigo sky, whipping him on like the reason why.

BECAUSE I'M A VOODOO CHILE...I'M A VOODOO CHILE...

Pathways formed to the edge of night, and Zeno knew that he had entered a new phase and a new depth. A curving, colonnaded avenue, that was perhaps some mighty fragment of the giant helix, formed an ascending avenue before him. Zeno had never previously been taken so far...or so far out... ever rising, born by divine and endlessly present Fender sustain to the very thresholds of nucleotide species memory. Far below, the simple nerve end, twelve bar, call and response of pain and pleasure were laid out like an abandoned landscape, obsolete in its restricted dimension and too mundane to be relevant. Shots of argon electricity, however, joy jolted the length of his macro extended perception, way beyond any know event horizon, stimulant packaged in tune with the relentless bass and percussion. Ooooh, and he could still groan and luxuriate. Animal responses were in no way a memory, present, but heightened and transfigured. (The Black Avenger covered all. Bases.) And, as if to remind him that, at no time, should anything be taken too seriously, a Bugs Bunny sign appeared between a pair of columns that posed a simple single question.

TRIPPIN' YET?

The colonnade wound to a cypress grove where the ancient gods waited to admit him to the Nago Mysteries. The Goddess Erzulie occupied primary place in the lengthened square at the outer ring, wreathed in the sanctified altar smoke of the poteau-mitan that rose from the center of Hell to the center of the sky. In the formal style, she was attended

by Severine Belle-Femme, Doctor Hypodermic, Marassah
Guinin (the African Twins) and a congress of Holy Dwarves,
and the left hand of the Goddess was graced by the Elizabeth
Taylor diamond that would draw him towards its geometric
intrigues and ready him for conquering admission. In the
aurora flair at the Heart Of Darkness, grounded by the Iron
Spear, the Danbhalah (the Snake Creator) was long, seven
miles, laying the oum'phor that would provide can-zo for
Luci-Fer, the Evening Star, the fastidious Madame Charlotte
and the intractable Baron Samedi in the unmasking of the
Hoochie Coochie Man. (And Jim Morrison gave head to
Jimi in the Steve Paul's Scene in nineteen and sixty-nine.)

I SAID I DIDN'T MEAN TO TAKE UP ALL YOUR
SWEET TIME

I'LL GET RIGHT BACK ONE OF THESE DAYS

Zeno was through the Mysteries of the Nago. Breaking out
from the final, transparent, blue-lightning-veined helical
egg, Zeno was beyond gender but held to a condition of
continuous orgasm at the same time as playing forty-seven
simultaneous chess games on a perpetual checkered board.
Guede Z'eclairs (The Lightning Bolts) flew beside him. Zeno
was one with the fullness of the program. No more. No less.
He had been touched by the Great God Legba and he would
feel no evil. He had outwitted the Beast and the Serpent of
the Pit and was beyond the reach of their talons. He had
irrevocably broken the seals and made exit of the monkey
world and could see no valid reason for return. The music
of the magnetic fields could continue world without end.
Amen. Amen.

IF I DON'T MEET YOU NO MORE IN THIS WORLD

I'LL MEET YOU IN THE NEXT ONE, DON'T BE
LATE

The towers and the midnight lamps, the dreams and Dark
Knights of Gotham were before him. Zeno was being made
aware that a major choice was coming, but major choice was
no option in the skies of Euphoria where Deja Thoris and
Dale Arden waited. Guede Z'eclairs spun high, giving way
as the Fuji blimp swung majestically past, trailing a reprise

on the cry of the wind.

DON'T BE LATE!

Zeno was snagged in a downtown freeway, threatened by tire tracks of crosstown traffic. He ran naked and in panic before Chrysler Imperials, Stutz Bearcats and White Freightliners. The ten-lane transition was too sudden and too gross. Guede Z'eclairs could not help him, The Lightning Bolts choked in the smoke, harried by helicopters of TV stations and police and the 7th Air Cavalry. His entire existence and experience was predicated on the giant flashing highway sign...the giant flashing highway sign... the giant flashing highway sign...

RIGHTHAND LANES MUST EXIT.

RIGHTHAND LANES MUST EXIT.

Zeno spun the wheel of the red Mustang screaming hard left across six lanes of hostile traffic. (The Black Avenger would have him. Do nothing else.) No way was he getting off this road. No way was he getting off this road. No way was he getting off this road. And his voice was Jimi's!

I'M A VOODOO CHILE. YEAH, I'M A VOODOO CHILE.

YEAH, I'M A VOODOO CHILE.

The exit ramp dropped away beside him and the road ahead was clear and endless. He had made return. He had rejected the Alpha jerk ejection. The Mustang picked up speed and blurred, finally dissolving. The Lightning Bolts were bearing him up. In clear blip of renewal, Granny Goodness gummed her pipe, as the world faded and restarted.

DON'T BE LATE!

DON'T BE LATE!

DON'T BE LATE!

DON'T BE LATE!

DON'T BE LATE!

DON'T BE LATE!

DON'T BE LATE!

The first move on the part of the paramedics was to pull the plug on Zeno. They knew, from the point of view of the patient, it was probably the worst possible course of action. A sudden unfiltered surge, an entire system buffering and backing up, as emergency power cells were stretched to their limits to preserve the most basic pattern enclosures. And then darkness. But what the fuck did they care? On their paychecks, they were supposed to risk raw voltage by trying to bring the asshole out easy? Worthless fucking shut-in shit jacked to black software. Fuck you, otaku. Bodybag the bastard and get the hell out of there. Let them hang him on a drip in the ER, he wouldn't be talking. Ever.

Written 1995. First published in the same year in the collection The Ultimate Experience, *edited by Chris Salewicz.*

That Johnny Ace is a hero may be open to some debate. To play Russian Roulette in the dressing room and lose is hardly heroism, although it did seem to suffice for Christopher Walken in *The Deerhunter,* notwithstanding that he was a consistent winner. Perhaps, in clarification, I should borrow a line from Howard Stern that was originally applied to his sidekick Stuttering John. Johnny Ace was a Hero of the Stupid.

JOHNNY ACE CAN'T LOSE

Pledging my love, baby
Johnny Ace can't lose

Spin the cylinder, Johnny
A universe of probability
And the curvature of time
Trapped in the rifled darkness
Between the foresight and the chamber
A darkness so milled to precision

That not even God could penetrate and find you
And even on Christmas Eve
Read the secrets of your soul

Pledging my love, baby,
Johnny Ace can't lose

Spin the cylinder, Johnny
You spent a full five days
Adjusting the exact acute angle
Of the yellow feather
In the watered silk band of your black Borsolino
But you haven't messed with
The three-and-a-half pound pull
On the trigger
On the Smith and Wesson model 29
Leaving it as it came from the box
Virgin and uncustomized
A cherry piece
Clear to the moment that
You put it upside your head

Pledging my love, baby
Johnny Ace can't lose

Spin the cylinder, Johnny
Firm hands above a cigarette scarred table
In a backstage dressing room
At the Houston Civic Auditorium
Where the show is over
And the lights are all turned out
And the black hat stands beside
A fifth of Kentucky Colonel
And in another part of the building
Perry Como is singing "silent night, holy night"
On the janitor's radio
And over in Memphis
Elvis Presley is delivering electrical goods

Or gift wrapping presents for his mom

Pledging my love, baby
Johnny Ace can't lose

Spin the cylinder, Johnny
The women are waiting, homes
There's three of them down the hallway
And they don't look like they're inclined
To wait all night
Particularly on your sorry
Doctor Saturday, death wish ass
I'm telling you, man
There's this fine young thing
I'm talking fine prime
All the time
She got this leopardskin dress
So tight it don't need no imagining
Like Etta James or Innez Foxx
And her sister has a back on her
That could make a Texas Ranger
Weep on a Sunday morning
And lips that look as though
They would never up and quit on a man
Any time through the duration
So work the magic act, jack
Come on through that dark place
Of wolfman howling and silver projectiles
Hit that oiled and mechanized hollow click
Roll the six to one shot, John
And let's get the hell out of here

Pledging my love, baby
Johnny Ace can't lose

Written 1996, never previously published.

Gene Vincent might also be categorized as another Hero of the Stupid, drinking and pilling himself to death in his very early thirties, and sobbing for his mother as he coughed up his bleeding guts in the trailer park, but, after Count Dracula, he was one of my earliest role models, so fuck off. Gene was the white punk from the pool hall, the greasy teen who would one day be corrupted and bowdlerized into Fonzie. Ian Dury made it clear there was one in every town. I so desperately wanted to be the one in my town, and who can tell in such long retrospect? Maybe I was. They certainly ran me out at an early enough age.

THE LONESOME DEATH OF GENE VINCENT

Oh Mama, oh Mama
This time I'm going down for sure
This time I'm going to hell
Like they always said I would

My ulcer's bleeding
And my bad leg's hurting
And the whiskey ain't helping
And the morphine don't make a dent
And outside this trailer
There's a world that I don't understand

They changed the rules, Mama
They took the fins off the cars
And Jim Boy Morrison is wearing my old clothes
And it's 1971, Mama, not 1957
And Be-Bop-A-Lula's on welfare, Mama
With two ugly kids and a bottle of 'ludes
Hustling truckers outside of Bakersfield
The dark cab of a White Freightliner

Ten bucks for a blowjob
And watch out for the gearshift baby
And you just watch out there, you hear

There's a smoke cloud rising, Mama
And it's clouding up my head
Lucky Strike Plain
In the old red and white pack
And the others are calling, Mama
The ones who went before
Hank Williams is whispering
Hank says he wants to buy this kid a drink
And Eddie Cochran's got a new tune
That he wants to play me on his black guitar

I gotta go, Mama
I gotta go soon
There's a woman waiting
With a red dress on
That old Whore of Babylon
Waiting to lay me down
That old Whore of Babylon
Wanting to take me down

I swear, Mama
I swear before God
If I get through this
I'm going to be a better man
Kick is though, Mama
I ain't gonna get through this
Kick is though, Mama
Already I can feel the ulcer ripping
Kick is though, Mama
Already I can taste the blood
I used to be a king, Mama
I used to be a king
The Demon King
King of the fucking Jungle

And they kept me in a cage
I reminded them of too much
Said I was drunk on *American Bandstand*
Said I was a communist
Run out of the world by Dick Clark
And a bunch of assholes called Bobby

I used to have Cadillacs, Mama
You ever hear of a communist with Cadillacs?
A Caddy for every day of the week
And a white Corvette on Sundays
But now
There's only one Cadillac left for me
And that's the long black rubber
Tired hearse, Mama
That's the only Cadillac in my future
The graveyard's out by the freeway, Mama
Out on some land that ought to be desert
If they didn't keep the sprinklers running
Twenty-three hours a day
The graveyard's out by the freeway, Mama
And the graveyard's hard to miss
Just take a left and follow the smell of diesel
All the way down the one one eight
And across the Ventura county line

Oh, Mama, oh Mama, you can't miss the graveyard
You sure as shit can't miss the graveyard

Written 1992, first published 1995.

Doc Holliday had bad lungs and an opium habit, and he was always my favorite Western gunfighter. Languid, literate, alcoholic, well-mannered, bad-tempered, played Chopin badly, but dressed to kill in shades of grey and a patch of color, and apparently

had little regard for human life, most especially his
own. What more can an exile tubercular gentleman
ask when fallen on five card stud and the kindness
of desperadoes in a silver mine called Tombstone,
except maybe for the attentions of Big Nose Kate, and
the occasional gunfight to break the ennui?

IS THERE A CHINAMAN IN TOWN?

Is there a Chinaman in town?

Doc always asked the same question
As the room fell silent
At the ponderous tread of his bootheels
Down the length of the hardwood floor
And the slight creak of his damaged lungs
Every eye covertly upon him
And there wasn't a saloon in the territory
Where at least one barfly asshole
Didn't recognize him for who he was
And whisper it to the others

Is there a Chinaman in town?

Doc always asked the same question
A slow survey of the interior
Never turning his back
On the sunlight leaking through the door
And the gawkers would avert their eyes
Through three fast shots of bourbon
Like his life depended on them
His hands shook slightly
As he pulled off his gloves
But then he'd fix the bartender
With a stare that could freeze gin

Is there a Chinaman in town?

They all knew what Doc meant
They all knew what Doc needed
Was there a room with a secret door
That led through the Portal of Time
To the Palace of Mirrors?
Was there a hidden place
Behind the laundry
Knock three times and say
That Woo sent me?

Is there a Chinaman in town?

Is there a place where men
Racked and inert
Could dream the dream?
Is there a place
Of sweet smoke and glowing coals?
A long pipe and a cooling fan?
Is there a place of silent safety
Where the tail of the dragon
Will finally come to rest?

Is there a Chinaman in town?

Can anyone direct me
To the solitude of divine night
To the chamber of shadows
Where legend can be laid to rest
Along with all the reproaching ghosts
Is there an enclosure
Of small death and brilliant images
Where memory stills
With the flask of laudanum
Beyond the reach of the bodies and the old perfume
And I am no longer required to listen
To the echoes of dead men's pistol shots

Is there a Chinaman in town?

Samuel Taylor Coleridge
Thomas de Quincy
Doc Holliday
Please tell me, gentlemen

Is there a Chinaman in town?

Written 1994. Recorded 1995 as a demo with Jack Lancaster and Wayne Kramer. Released as part of a CD collection of Deviants and Pink Fairies outtakes The Silence of the Hams.

The entire matter of heroes, role models and admiration in general also carries its own weight of disillusionment and disappointment.

ENVY

I used to envy Elvis but then he got fat and died
I used to envy Marlon Brando but then he got fat and his
    kid died
I used to envy Jim Morrison but then I got out of the bath
    tub
Now I don't envy anyone
It causes bloating
And far too many funerals

Written 1994. Recorded 1995 with Jack Lancaster for the CD The Deathray Tapes, *released 1995 by Alive Records, Los Angeles.*

Naturally all else pales beside the kind of protracted courage that is totally impossible to imagine or even guess at.

THE RED OCTOBER TRACTOR FACTORY

Whenever I hit one of the sloughs of depression and despondency that make artists such a pain in the ass to be around, I remind myself of the two Russian soldiers who, during the World War II siege of Stalingrad, manned a machine gun nest in the Red October Tractor Factory for 52 straight days, frequently starving and always freezing. I mean, how can that determination and suffering be compared to, say, the fear of creative failure or the pangs of unrequited love? And yet maybe one or both of them, in another time and another place, ached for a lost love to the point of suicidal contemplation. Which, of course, begs the question can pain, or joy for that matter, ever be quantified?

Written 2000, never previously published.

AND NOW FOR THE CARTOONS

At risk of sounding like Krusty the Klown, there now follows a short graphic interlude. In the nineteen seventies, I was heavily involved in both the scripting and publishing of what were then known as underground comics. Indeed, I was involved to the point, in fact, that in 1973, the authorities in the United Kingdom took it upon themselves to prosecute me to the full extent of the law for the crime of publishing the work of cartoonist Robert Crumb in a comic book that I edited titled *Nasty Tales*, and I was forced, along with my partners in the alleged crime, to spend ten less than pleasant days on trial at London's Old Bailey. Fortunately for my health, liberty, and sanity, a jury of my peers agreed that there was no intrinsic harm in the supposedly offending material, and I was allowed to go free without a stain on my character.

The following pages originally appeared in a book put out in 1975 by Kosmik Komiks titled *Rock & Roll Madness*. It was conceived a full two years before the death of Elvis Presley, at a time when the King of Rock & Roll was in major downer and rhinestone decline, and we all wondered what the hell he was going to do next. The fantasy may had been a little cruel, but we weren't terribly pleased with Elvis Aaron at the time. Illustrator Dave Gibbons would later go on to find graphic fame drawing *Judge Dredd* and other mainstream hits. These pages are reproduced with his permission.

Vince Eugene's humble start in Hogwallow, Georgia, is now a legend...

How he grew up a healthy, average American boy...

LOOKIT TH' JUGS ON THAT ONE!

How, even at an early age, a certain something set young Vince apart from the other kids...

HEY, VINCE, YOU COMIN' OUT TO NIGGERTOWN TO WHUP SOME COONS?

PLINK PLONK

PARP PARP

SCREECH!

NOPE – I'M GONNA SET HERE A SPELL AN' PLAY MUH GEETAR!

FUNNY MUTHA, THAT VINCE.

VROOOOM!

PLUNK PLUNK

1957 was the year it all happened. With his first record, Lonesome Convertible, Vince Eugene topped charts all over the world...

He followed that with other successes like Mess You Up, Killed My Buddy and Eighteen Car Pileup...

Vince Eugene became the greatest rock star the world had ever seen...

It was in 1976 that Vince Eugene's career moved into yet another field...

GO GO GO WITH TED

GOGO WITH VINCE AND

TEDDY

I give you my running mate and the next vice-president of the U.S.A. --Vince Eugene!

GO GO

Then...in Atlanta, before a crowd of thousands, tragedy struck...

Herald

PRESI

ASSA

The full weight of the presidency fell on Vince. He took the oath of office on his live T.V. spectacular.

VE

VE

Yuh done a good job, Vito...

Come on over and pick up your hundred grand.

81

MUH FELLOW 'MERICANS...

As president, he was quick to act to restore order to a country shattered by grief...

With lightning intuition, he abolished the constitution, dissolved congress and declared himself president for life...

THAT ABOUT WRAPS IT UP, VITO...

WELL, FOLKS, THAT'S THE STORY OF VINCE EUGENE, IT HAS BEEN AN HONOUR IN THESE FEW PAGES TO PAY OUR TRIBUTE TO A TRULY GREAT MAN.

DON'T MISS NEXT WEEK'S MEN OF DESTINY, WHEN WE FEATURE...

RUPERT MURDOCH

THE MAN WHO SAVED THE ENGLISH LANGUAGE!

Pit-stops to Perdition

In those days in the New York 1980s, when Henry Cabot Beck and I wrote and composed for our band Tijuana Bible, along with, at various times, Victoria Rose, John Collins and Pablo, the fliers for our live shows frequently began with the preamble, "If the Good Lord's willing and the creek don't rise..." This conceit was also an homage to the poster for Hank Williams' last show, the gig which Hank never made because he died in the back of the Caddy on the way there. We liked to pretend we were on some great Lost Highway where every event-horizon was just another pit-stop to perdition. With our poems and our electric guitars, we walked the Earth like Kane, except the Earth we walked was pretty much confined to a rectangular area south of Houston Street and north of Canal, although one time Henry and I did take the show to Europe.

In our imaginations, on the other hand, we could transport ourselves, and sometimes the audience, anywhere we wanted, and the Lost Highway could take us clear into Hunter S. Thompson's Bat Country in grail-search for Elvis, the Holy Shaman, and the psychedelics of the damned. This piece also shows the revision to the mystic (dead) Elvis of the 1990's from the somewhat more dubious (live) Elvis of the early 1970s.

MEMPHIS PSYCHOSIS

I was running fast on I 61
Maybe three hours outside of Memphis
Making good time and driving smooth
On course for the Elvis Presley
Souvenir shopping mall and pharmacy

It was only a '51 Hudson
But it was running like a dream
And about the only thing
That stopped it being a perfect day
Was that I couldn't get anything
On the radio
But Bobby Rydell, G. Gordon Liddy
Or Oral Roberts
Who was threatening to strike me dead
If I didn't send him money

All in all though
I was feeling pretty good
Which made it come as a major surprise that I
Never made it to Memphis

It was probably my own fault
I should never have taken those pills
That were offered in the men's room
By a Mexican in a lime green matador suit
That not even the Artist Formally Known As Prince
Would have the gall to wear

We were in this Denny's
Somewhere along the way
I'd only pulled in for a cup of coffee
A pack of cigarettes
And some Jim Thompson fantasy about the waitress

The Mexican wanted five bucks a pop for these suckers
Maybe I shouldn't have taken ten
But I was in the mood for conspicuous consumption
And the ghost of Elvis was at my shoulder
I should have suspected that something was up
When he made a secret handsignal
And vanished
Carlos Castaneda comes in all shapes and sizes

Even then, though, there on the parking lot
Beside this pink and black twelve-wheeler
With chromium trim
Hauling frozen chickens to Shreveport, Louisiana
I never thought that I wouldn't make it to Memphis

I guess it all really started
With the flickerings at the corners of my eyes
That I dismissed at the time
As being a result of having
Not slept for forty-eight hours straight

The bats came later

At first they were content
To loiter in the periphery of my vision
But, after a while,
They got real, real bold
And started flying alongside the car
In formation
Like they were on their way to bomb Dresden

It got really bad
When I was going down
This slight incline
There wasn't another car in sight
And then I ran into this waist deep
Hammer horror,

Edgar Allen Poe mist
And began to realize that
I wasn't going to make it to Memphis

Now after I hit the mist
All I could get on the radio
Was this angelic choir

And now the signs are written in Assyrian
And, at any moment, Rod Serling
Is going to come marching through the windshield
And offer me for your consideration

Oh God! Oh Graceland!
Am I in a lot of trouble
I have lost all sense of motion
And my hands are turning blue
And there's definitely
Something wrong with space and time
And the Hudson has started to glow

Oh shit...here comes the monolith

What did I do
To finish up here
As some post-Einstein zombie Flying Dutchman
In a wormhole that I can't get out of
Because, in here, there's no such concept as out
Life's a bitch and then you're infinite
And I never made it to Memphis

Written 1988. Recorded 1993 by Tijuana Bible on the CD Gringo Madness *released 1993 by Big Beat Records, London. Recorded again in 1995 with Jack Lancaster for the CD* The Deathray Tapes, *released 1995 by Alive Records, Los Angeles. A live version was included on the compilation* Son Of Ham, *and the piece was covered by Tohuwabohu on their album* Empty and Senseless.

I have lodged in a great many hotels in my time, from the grand to the indescribable and even The Chelsea on 23rd Street. It has been my observation that all hotels come with a measure of unreality; a mint on the pillow and pornography on the TV, or a neon sign that turns the ceiling bloody and empty crack vials in a drawer with the Gideon Bible. Both come with sounds that cannot be identified, and lend one to Stedi-cam hallucinations of Caligari corridors, and listening out for the presence and thoughts of all the unseen others, wondering who is doing god-knows-what in the isolation of their cubes of space, and, after that speculation is worn thin, trying to decipher the soft whispering of the electricity in the wires.

THE LEADER HOTEL

The desk clerk weighs in about five hundred pounds
He got the latest issue of *Gagged And Bound*
There never was no bell hop, don't think about the bell
You carry your own luggage at the Leader Hotel

Tenth floor burned-out minor rockstar, TV broke and drinking gin
The money ran out long ago and the snakeskin's wearing thin
And the women just get weirder, no more magic in their spell
He's a prisoner of entropy in the Leader Hotel

Bass boost Michael Jackson to cover up the screams
As Peggy Sue for payment peddles noire dreams
Two hundred dollar ticket for a round trip tour of hell

Peggy Sue pays her rent at the Leader Hotel

Mail order scopesight rifle in a shiny rexene case
And now he's got to shoot someone or else be losing face
He's Lee Harvey Oswald in his tiny top floor hell
Ammunition's a condition at the Leader Hotel

They manufacture xstasy, they manufacture bombs
There's *Alien* on the VCR and his girlfriend wearing
    thongs
Whichever way you slice it it's only buy or sell
The action is transactional at the Leader Hotel

Next door there is the Terminal Bar which is where the
    terminal go
W.C. Fields hanging out with G.I. Joe
You can make it for a while though you may not feel so
    well
The drinking stops you thinking at the Leader Hotel

There's the faintest smell of mildew or maybe turpentine
Green bottle in the garbage black label Night Train wine
And each transparent victim is hardening her shell
Survival is an art form at the Leader Hotel

There's Cubans with machine guns and Colombians with
    drugs
And girls who live life dangerously by shacking up with
    thugs
The shell-shocked and the shocking with tales they'll never
    tell
Down at the end of Lonely Street, that's the Leader Hotel

*Written 1987. Recorded in the same year with Tijuana Bible
for the CD* Gringo Madness, *released by Big Beat, London
1993.*

The first time I went to Mexico I experienced an odd sense of disappointment, which took me a while to figure out. I finally realized that my problem was that I didn't want to be in Mexico in the late twentieth century. I was about eighty years too late for the good stuff.

THE MOVEMENTS OF THE WHORES ON REVOLUTION PLAZA

On a warm night he'd take his drink to the terrace
And watch the movements of the whores on Revolution
   Plaza

For half the price of a cocktail drunk, a swaying parade of
   tattered finery
A cheap fur over white nudity, a covert flash of cheap
   lingerie
A hot pitch for cold comfort and a straight edge razor in
   an evil hour

He'd observe with interest the petite blonde in the short
   ruffled dress
And the Phillydog bouffant
The girl who had a near phobic hatred of priests and nuns
And all of the obvious officers of organized religion
And who would spit on them as they passed
"You think God's got nothing better to do with his time
Than brood on who gets laid and how?"
He'd wonder at the huge woman who practiced subjugation
In corset and lace, beckoning imperiously to her tricks
With a cruel cool crooked finger
Insisting that they follow, meek heads bowed
Five discreet paces behind
Up the outside staircase that led to the second floor room
With the hell scarlet wallpaper

He never let himself be caught looking at the Oriental tiny
    girl in the rubber skirt
She was too tightly wrapped for casual inspection
And he had been told about her reputation for switchblade
    hostility
And her taste for the pipe
And the pearl-handled .22 she carried in her shoulderbag

For half the price of a cocktail drunk, a swaying parade of
    tattered finery
A cheap fur over white nudity, a covert flash of cheap
    lingerie
A hot pitch for cold comfort and a straightedge razor in an
    evil hour

On a warm night he'd take his drink to the terrace
And watch the movements of the whores on Revolution
    Plaza

*Written 1993. Recorded in the same year with Tijuana Bible
for the CD* Gringo Madness, *released by Big Beat, London
1993.*

Two Tales of Heads for Sale

Humanity has always been fascinated by the idea of the disembodied head. Put a price on his head. Bring me the head of Alfredo Garcia. The heads of traitors were displayed on the spikes of pikes, above the gates of the city. In British stately homes, decapitated ghosts haunt-walk with their heads tucked underneath their arms. The head is the container which carries the eyes and the brain. It is from the head that we look out on the world, and it is apparently the place where we do our thinking. The inevitable projection is that the head can somehow survive the body and come out the other side of death with personality, skills, and memory intact, and if the power and nutrients could be restored, the head could once more live. Ideally in the service, or at the mercy of its resuscitator.

What follows owes much to the 1963 film *They Saved Hitler's Brain.*

VINNIE WANTS TO SELL ME HITLER'S BRAIN

I had lost four days in New Jersey to an industrial wasteland of drink and drugs//And time-dated metal girls, stumbling barbiturate harlots//Who imagined they were bit players in some Bruce Springsteen fantasy//Of lost but untamed youth//And now I was going back to face the music//

In fever yellow, New York summer dawn, the lull before the Bladerunner heat//Light between the Chrysler Building and the Empire State//Across in the Manhattan haze beyond the George Washington bridge//And I know that I have to have just one more drink before I total my future

There's just one place that I know for certain is open//A Little Italy, bentnose goomba//After hours, joint-with-no-name on Elizabeth Street//With a stuffed and varnished marlin on the wall// And a signed picture of Frank Sinatra//With his arm around the owner//And the only reason they let me in and sell me booze at any hour of the day or night//Is that the owner's wife believes crazy people bring good luck

So I order a shot and sink on a stool//Not even caring that the only thing the jukebox seems able to play//Is Dean Martin singing "Volare"//Oh-oh-oh//And then I perceive a broad back in a black silk shirt//Bent over the old Gottleib "Hot Pursuit" pinball machine//And I am aware that this back belongs to (Oh yeah) Vinnie Coagulino//And I know that it is too late to leave//And I cannot skulk away without the action being considered a considerable gesture of disrespect

I am not exactly proud to number Vinnie Coagulino among my acquaintances//Although, at times, the very mention of his name has put more than one overtly aggressive fool//Into soft focus//Vinnie Coagulino is a bad man//A raging bull without restraint or finesse//And he enters a room as though Ennio Morricone//Was playing in his head//And when he turns and spots me, I feel a little soft focus myself//"Yo, Mikey"//Vinnie always calls me Mikey//I dislike it but that's not the kind of thing you tell to Vinnie//"You keeping out of trouble? When you gonna quite that writing shit and get a job?"//Hardy-har, Vinnie, very droll//In Vinnie's estimation, he's the funniest sonofabitch since Don Rickles//And where Vinnie is, it's Vinnie's estimation that counts

"Come out to the car, kid, I got something to show you"//My

heart sinks, when Vinnie invites you out to the car, a number of options can exist//He either wants to sell you some hot cashmere sweaters//Or you may never be seen again except as part of a crime scene photo//Face down in the marshgrass outside of Newark//Out in the street, Vinnie opens the trunk of his '87 Continental//And lifts out a black plastic Hefty bag//"Maybe you get a kick out of this, Mikey"//
I peek into the bag//Something lurks, dark and sloshing, a rotting cauliflower in bloody liquid// I get no kick, but Vinnie grins, exhibiting a 22-carat dental job//"A human brain, Mikey"

Oh god — Dahmerland//Reality as a shallow grave//"But no ordinary human brain, Mikey, the carefully preserved brain of Adolf Hitler"//In my condition, I have no doubt that Vinnie speaks the absolute truth

The universe reels and evil forcefields stream in from hexed nebuli//Black holes pulse as they traverse malign redshifts// Suns pale and fixed points slide out of alignment//And for a whole nanosecond, the entire matrix is off line//Motherships falter in their courses, three-headed reindeer are born in Lapland and milk sours//Vinnie is attempting to sell me Hitler's brain//As the universe was reeling and the black holes pulsing//Vinnie was explaining//How he had come by such a significant organ//Something about the Vatican and the KGB and a deep dark vault under the basilica of St. Peter's//That Vinnie had somehow managed to pillage

It was maybe the result of a dysfunctional childhood//But I'm going for it//Or maybe it was the four days I lost in Jersey// But I'm going for it//Maybe because I know all the legends// I'm going for it//What should have been the money for the phone company changes hands//I'm going for it//I'm going for it so hard that I hardly heed Vinnie's final warning//"It don't come with instructions, Mikey"

I know that all I have to do is to recreate the circuits//

93

Hardwire the dials and electrodes and flashing lights//And hook them to the big Tesla coil and the power is mine// The power unlimited is mine//The power unlimited//The power immeasurable//The power to make myself the Evil Dictator of the Universe//"It don't come with instructions, Mikey"//For the next eight weeks I scour discount electronics stores//From one end of Canal Street to the other//Seeking seemingly appropriate coils and condensers//Circuit boards and random sequencers in suitably garish colors//And polished steel discharge columns//I feel myself on the path to galactic autocracy//"It don't come with instructions, Mikey"

Finally the components are assembled and they look good// They look real, real good considering I'm working without a manual//"It don't come with instructions, Mikey"//I apply the power//Lights dim//Like an execution in the big house//Domestic TV pictures strobe and roll//As far south as Battery Park and as far north as 15th Street//In my basement, the Tesla coil cascades purple static//And the brain begins to move//The brain ripples with crawling life//It spasms//It shudders//And a dull glow begins to suffuse its very core// It nervously vibrates as though waking from an eternal nightmare//I take a deep breath//I have drawn Excalibur from the stone//I am ready to take the power unto myself

Then — phut!

A tube blows//The Tesla coil dims//The brain ceases to crawl and becomes flaccid//All motion stops//Vibration ceases// Dead//Still//Silence//"It don't come with instructions, Mikey"// The smell of burnt insulation and organic rot fills the basement//And all down Seventh Avenue// TV pictures return to normal reruns of *The Honeymooners*//I have failed, the brain will never move again//I will never be Evil Dictator of the Universe//And it will take a lot of time and a lot of gin to get over this disappointment

First improvised 1987. Never previously published in this form.

Same idea, different context. The severed head remains the repository of the evil nuclear core and all the memory and the dark data applicable to that evil. Again, all of this is wholly accessible to anyone with the necessary magic, mechanisms or software; all three being, for these purposes, pretty much interchangeable. In the previous poem the protagonists were Nazis and the Mob; this time around, I went for white trash drug addicts and the Knights Templar. All art is mix, match and infinite interchange.

HEAD 58 AND THE MANTIS SYNDROME

Inside of the next few hours, Byron knew he would either be dead or rich beyond his wildest dreams. As always, the crucial fulcrum was the goddamned degrees of separation. Once those sons of bitches started breaking down, there was no knowing where the flow was going to go. The dam became breached and all the superior man could do was attempt to surf the tide before it drowned him. Already, in room number 13, the box was starting to leak light under the door of the motel closet, enough to illuminate the mildew stains on the ceiling and the black velvet painting of Elvis on the wall above the bed. Luckily the woman was out cold. Explaining the box and its contents would be close to impossible, and he had forgotten the incantation that would stop Head 58 from glowing.

"Never in a million years, babe."

Explaining it to himself was almost impossible. Even when the eyes of Elvis were upon him. He looked down at the sleeping women. When he'd spoken, she had stirred slightly but he knew she wouldn't be roused. Too much tequila, followed by prolonged and less than conventional sex, and she would probably sleep until well past noon. Then she'd wake, almost certainly wishing she hadn't. Of course, by noon, they might both be past wishing. They might both actually be dead. It depended who got there first.

The right hand path in this deadly Vegas crapshoot – the white light of goodness in this if-the-yin-don't-get-you-the-yang-will – was the least complicated of the two. That was the three-some million dollars that would be handed to him in simple transaction for the box and its contents. Perhaps white light of goodness was pushing the metaphor to its outer limit, but you could hardly describe a Mormon security bagman on high-priced loan from the spook strata of the Church of Latter Day Saints as a disciple of the dark side. Not in this context, Jack. Sure the faceless nameless billionaire with the lease on the operative might well be the Lord Abraxis incarnate, but anyone who was prepared to let him walk out of the Flying Saucer Martian Motor Court, out here in the middle of the haunted, wind-deviled Mojave Desert, alive and an at least temporary millionaire, could only be viewed as the good guy. Particularly when the horror of the opposition was figured into the equation.

"That's right. The opposition." Byron's voice had taken on the sound of a man who was not facing the unfaceable or thinking the unthinkable only because he had blanked his brain and turned away from reality. If the opposition were to get to him before the Mormon, the hideousness would not be limited to any speedy homicide. By this point, he was well aware that he was dealing with a subspecies who would take a deep dark glee in cat and mousing him to perverse agony before the fatal finale. The best hiding place that Byron could find was in a total concentration on the motel and the moment.

The Flying Saucer Martian Motor Court was a failed UFO tourist trap, with supremely trashy Ed Wood architecture and science fiction neon. It stood some forty mesquite miles in the wrong direction along what is laughingly known as

Route 375 from downtown Rachel, Nevada, too far from the periphery of Dreamland to ever make any commercial nut bucks from the seekers after aliens.

He had questioned Ten Day Gene about both the Mormon and The Flying Saucer Martian Motel. On the subject of the Mormon, Ten Day Gene had only smiled, despite the fact that he was hemorrhaging to death. "They're the last ones you can still trust, those Salt Lake City Angels of Death. They still think of it as just a business." In the matter of the motel, the smile had faded to be replaced by a shrug and a wince. "It's known to those who know. Although it has little to recommend it, but, either way, you won't be there very long."

His entire predicament was, of course, all the fault of Ten Day Gene.

The adventure, or maybe the crisis, a matter of perspective either way, had begun when Ten Day Gene had come clawing at his door. The door in question was to Byron's low rent, East Hollywood, outside walkup, with the steel stairs like a cheap Central American prison painted pink, where the manager, a full-blood Aleut Indian, sprinkled crushed Pall Malls in front of the car port to ward off the coyotes. Gene had been less than coherent, and the story had been hard to piece together. Ten Day Gene was named because, reputedly, he only slept once every ten days. When he was younger, Ten Day Gene had been such a formidably creative sociopath that he had been more than capable of scaring Harley trash, road rat bikers into mutely confused submission. And it was no way on account of his size. Oh no. Ten Day Gene was, in fact, small, feral and ferret-like, but, to compensate for this, he never went anywhere without at least four lethal weapons concealed about his black-clad body, the standard Glock or Desert Eagle in a clamshell shoulder holster under the Doc Holliday frock coat, plus butterfly knives and strange Oriental devices from the outer limits of the martial arts, the use of which he took a positive delight in demonstrating under actual field conditions. He was also reputed to carry a wallet-size slab of fully fused Semtex as a piece of personal mutually-assured destruction, should the shit really go south.

The first inkling all was not as it should be with Gene was when the frock coat fell open revealing that he'd received a nasty cut across the lower thorax from what appeared to be a chainsaw. He had slumped into the nearest chair and, after demanding whiskey, let out a close to terminal wheeze as blood leaked down his zoot peggies. "I hate to tell you, my good and faithful companion, but the next sound I hear might well be the Fat Lady's aria."

Ten Day Gene talked in his own unique mixture of B-movie dialogue and John Fennimore Cooper, but, right at the moment he was having trouble talking at all. The tale was told in fits and starts, between groans of pain and hits on the quart of Wild Turkey that Byron had pressed into his shaking hands. As far as Byron could follow the disjointed narrative, Gene had pushed the envelope a tad too far and one time too many. He had allowed himself to be hired on for cold cash and a taste of the profits by a crew of ex-Aryan Brotherhood, genetically-challenged trailer park inbreds, to oversee an extra-legal methamphetamine transaction they were in the process of negotiating with some of the hard inner core of a Nyarlathotep-worshiping Cthulhu-related proto-cult, who not only funded their activities by the sale of ex-agrichemical oil drum crank, but also used the stuff as an early adjunct to the luredom of their prospective thralls.

Seemingly these cultists had decided to revise the protocols of trade, and business had degenerated into a rapid hail of gunfire and the snare of the aforementioned chainsaw. Even Ten Day Gene was taken somewhat by surprise. "I guess I should have known better. I mean, those sons of bitches are unpredictable by definition. Them bringing the Head with them should have tipped me off to the way it would go down, except I didn't find out about the Head until the echoes faded and the smoke was hanging and everyone except yours truly was dead, ripped and bloody on the floor. And I wasn't feeling too well myself after the brush with the chainsaw. It was only while I was sitting a moment, gathering my wits prior to lamming out of there, that I saw the accursed thing, glowing slightly with a smug blue light, on account of all the death moment energy still lingering in the room. Somehow the box it came in had been pushed under the coffee table, out of sight, unless one was, as I, sagging low on the couch. A big old Victorian leather hatbox, it was, worn and stained, the kind with a handle and a single strap across the top. Needless to say, my first instinct was to take a look. As I moved it, the glow winked out. Presumably as the dread thing realized that it had been observed. On first inspection, as I lifted the lid, it looked like nothing more than a somewhat venerable human head, repeatedly varnished and pickled over the centuries. Arcane and unusual perhaps, but far from inconceivable remembering the nature of those who had brought it. I guess having just debatably escaped a lethal drug massacre, my intellect wasn't functioning with anything like its usual acuity, and it took me a few moments before it came to me that I was, in fact, looking at the legendary Head 58, and much of what I had assumed to be a part of the preservation process was in fact the residue of the constant flow of what, in the thirteenth century, had been called the Holy Fire, but was now known to be simple ecto-flux plasma, if ecto-flux plasma could ever be described as simple."

For one so close to the great dark divide, Ten Day Gene took some quite literal pains to tell the story and clarify the situation as fully as he could. Seemingly some debate existed over the true origin of Head 58. Some claimed it to be that of Hassan-a-Sabbah, the Old Man of the Mountains and instigator of the Hashasheens. Others insisted it was the head of Abdul Alhazred, the so-called "Mad Arab" who was alleged to have authored the *Necronomicon*. A third school of thought suggested the head belonged to Baybar the Mameluke who sacked Acre in 1291. A small but vocal faction insisted the Head was far older, being the sole physical remnant of a human/alien hybrid left behind after the Nephilim nuked the Cities of the Plain. According to legend, up to around 1900, Head 58 had been the jealously guarded power source and central devotional object of the

Order of Knights Templar.

According to Ten Day Gene, when the Templars were ripped by early 20th century internal conflict, the Head had somehow been lost. Passing from hand to hand, it had been briefly possessed by, among others, J.P. Morgan, T.E. Lawrence, Jean Cocteau, King Farouk, Heinrich Himmler, the Duke of Windsor, Chiang Kai-shek, Howard Hughes, and a well known rock & roll star who had publicly and repeatedly claimed to be a follower of Aleister Crowley. It would seem, however, that not one of them had a true understanding of the power or potential of Head 58. If they had, it never would have managed to cut itself loose and end up being dragged to a speed deal by a crew of knucklebrowed cultists who would precipitate a mass slaughter.

"For a while back there, I thought I might be able to get the thing to work for me. I knew, the way I was cut up, I wasn't going to live for more than a few hours without some fairly big-time intervention. And I was wondering if I could somehow activate the thing to get me up and moving. I remembered the story of James Wasserman, one of the Unholy Trinity who, after a session with the Head, was still going about his business like a large as life, living man, some five years after he had clinically died in front of a whole bunch of witnesses. Unfortunately, even concentrating to the max, I only managed to get a slight hum out of the head and a dull glow around the eyes. I guess I lacked the keys to the Masterlock because all I managed was enough power to make it as far as here."

It was probably fortunate that Byron was accustomed to being bemused, because, sure as shit, that was the way that Ten Day Gene's faltering monologue left him. Bemused, however, was replaced by alarm and concerned when Gene moved from ancient and modern history to the situation in the immediate present. "I stashed the Head in its hatbox outside your building, behind the garbage dumpsters."

"You did what?"

"I stashed the Head..."

"Yeah, yeah, I heard you. But why in hell did you do that?"

"Because they'll be coming for it."

Alarm now usurped confusion. "Who's coming for it?"

Ten Day Gene groaned. He was fading fast. "Actually it's two who's."

"Two?"

"There's two groups who seriously want to get their hands on the Head. On one side there's…"

Gene coughed blood and then, talking as quickly as he could, sketched out the story of the Mormon bagman, the anonymous billionaire and the three million dollars that would be handed over to Byron in return for the Head. "And the other group?"

"You ever heard of The Final Program Church of Methodology?"

"You mean the Methodologists? The ones who sell all those self help books? The ones who have the late night TV infomercials, and all those lamebrain movie stars giving them ten percent of their income?"

Gene took a hit of Wild Turkey and gasped. "That's just the surface level. It's the deep cover echelons…the fine focused true believers…who are coming after the Head."

"And how much are they gonna pay?"

"They won't pay nothing. They'll certainly kill whoever has the Head and probably lay a bad and extended ritual hurt on them before finally administering the coup de grace. Believe me, Byron, old friend, these cats are not only cut from the purest and most fundamental evil, but they really enjoy its indulgence."

"That's one fuck of a diversity of options."

Ten Day Gene made a noise that had to be a prelude to the death rattle. "Just look on me as your fickle finger of fate."

Back at the Flying Saucer Martian Motorcourt, the girl also made a small noise. Hers was partway between a whimper and a snore. Byron, in his nervous and hungover state, reflected on how maybe it hadn't been strictly ethical to bring her back to his room, but, in the nearby bar, by 1:00 A.M., they'd been drunk and she'd been more than willing. Bringing her to his room and his bed had also been strictly against Ten Day Gene's dying instructions. After telling Byron how he should rendezvous with the Mormon bagman out at the desert motel, he had issued two stern instructions. The first had been reasonably self-evident. "Trust no one. Keep yourself to yourself, no matter what." The second had been closer to the bizarre. "And, whatever you do, don't trust the Head. Head 58 has its own agenda. If it starts to glow, you can be pretty sure that it's going to do something inexplicable and exceedingly nasty. For fuck's sake use the incantation to put it back to sleep."

"The incantation?"

"Izizanimma ilani rabuti shima ya dababi."

"Izizanimma ilani rabuti shima ya dababi?"

"Remember it."

"Run it by me one more time."

But Ten Day Gene would run nothing by anyone ever again. In that very moment, he had died, slipping quietly into that dark night so gently that he hardly even twitched. With nothing to do but leave the mortal remains where they lay, with the quart of Wild Turkey still clutched in its cold dead fingers, Byron had hurried from the apartment. Retrieving the hatbox containing Head 58 from behind the dumpsters, he had climbed into his lime green, rattletrap Impala and set the Chevy heading for the I10 and ultimately the high desert, with a tape of The Stooges *Raw Power* blasting in an attempt to divert his attention, praying that both he and the car would complete the trip intact.

By an automotive near miracle, the Impala had made it all the way to the Flying Saucer Martian Motorcourt. After protracted flurry of motion and panic, all Byron could then do was to stash the Head in its hatbox and sit on the motel bed and await his fate, good or ill, with the black velvet painting of Elvis gazing down on him in a sideburned, lip-curled, cool reminder that this was one fine mess into which he had inadvertently placed himself. The situation was also not improved by the room being equipped with a TV that could only manage to pull in two snowy, interference blighted channels from out of Las Vegas, unless he deposited money.

In which case it would treat him to an in-house, Nevada porno channel that seemed to consist of highly gynecological close-ups, punctuated by commercials for a selection of the state's legalized whorehouses.

Within the space of two hours, the combination of all of the above had pushed Byron to the point where he was more than ready to ignore the dying strictures of the late Ten Day Gene to keep himself to himself, and drive the half hour to the cowboy roadhouse called Big Red's he had spotted on the way up. Big Red's was a shot and beer, back road attraction where loner desert rats came in to relieve the isolation and Marines from the desert training base at Twenty Nine Palms wound up when they'd been 86'd from everywhere else in a hundred square miles.

The girl hadn't exactly looked out of place in Big Red's. In a Rage Against The Machine T-shirt, punk black jeans, purple snakeskin cowboy boots and a Bettie Page fringe, drinking shots of tequila chased with a long necked Bud, she could have been some bohemian isolate out on the edge of the Mojave for her own mysterious reasons. Admitted she was considerably more attractive than the average desert isolate, and maybe he should have taken instinctive warning from that she was close-to-death pale in an environment where her skin should have been burned and dried to something close to old leather. Byron had no excuse for his lapse of street caution except that maybe the stress and circumstance of Ten Day Gene's dying request, and the subsequent race for the back of beyond, had scrambled his self-protective defenses. Another alternative was that she looked so good after all the horror that had gone before, and the potential horror that was yet to come, he had ceased to care. Her very attraction and the fact that, shortly after he walked into the place, and despite hostile stares from a couple of drugstore cowboys, she appeared also to be attracted to him, had robbed him of his reason.

Maybe another warning should have flashed up when, after little more than ninety minutes of booze and flirtation, she readily agreed to accompany him back to the Flying Saucer

Martian Motorcourt. Byron usually worked on the Groucho principle where strange women were concerned. The primary Marx Brother had actually said he "wouldn't want to belong to any club that would have me as a member," but Byron had always applied the same thesis to picking up women in bars. "Would you want to go home with any woman crazy enough to want to go home with you?" By this point, though, Byron was too far gone to worry about whether a strange woman might turn out to be crazy, particularly one with such inviting lips and breasts.

As she'd walked into room 13 at the Flying Saucer Martian Motorcourt, she'd looked round appraisingly. "Nice picture of Elvis. I always trust a motel room with a picture of Elvis. The same goes for Irish bars and Bobby Kennedy."

In sex, she had taken complete and complex control, but this caused Byron no problem. Quite the reverse, in fact. To simply relax and let some else make the running came as a blessed relief. Only in the wee hours of the morning, when the woman was asleep and the Head had started to glow, did he start to question both the wisdom and morality of bringing her there. Byron knew he had put himself on highly shaky ethical ground by gratuitously exposing a potential innocent bystander to the gruesomeness that might possibly be coming to his cabin door, but Byron had never been too ethically sound and such innate scruples as he might have possessed were easily overcome by lust and self interest. The glow of the Head, on the other hand, was something else again. Here ethics and self interest combined. Hadn't Ten Day Gene told him with his next-to-dying breath that, when the Head glowed, it was about to do something "inexplicable and exceedingly nasty." In this, both he and the pale dark-haired woman were both probably in clear and present danger, and he had to do something about it. He had to repeat the incantation. That's what Gene had said. Repeat the incantation if the Head started to glow. Except suddenly Byron's mind was a total blank. The incantation was gone, seemingly beyond recall.

"Izizanim..?" Was that the first word? It refused to come

back. The flight and the fear, the tequila and the beer, the prospect of sex and finally the consummating act of sex itself had all conspired to deprive him of his concentration.

"Izizanim..."

He could access nothing more than these three lame syllables and the Head was glowing more brightly by the moment. So focused was he on his dilemma that he completely failed to notice the dark-haired woman open her eyes. So far was she from his thoughts that he wasn't to the slightest degree aware when she slowly sat up, the sheets falling away from the breasts that he had earlier been licking and fondling. It was only when she spoke that he even remembered she was still in the bed. "Izizanimma ilani rabuti shima ya dababi."

The Head's glow diminished. The woman repeated the incantation. "Izizanimma ilani rabuti shima ya dababi."

The glow from under the closet door dimmed to nothing. Byron turned and looked at the woman in horror. "You knew the incantation?"

"I was waiting for you, wasn't I?"

Byron knew fear was hardly a quantitative or relative thing, but he was certain that he was more afraid than he'd ever been in his life before. "I suppose there's no chance you're a Mormon bringing me a lot of money?"

The woman's eyes were harder than any eyes that Byron could ever remember. Those eyes were never going to give him a break. She shook her head. "I'm not a Mormon."

Byron had no better idea than to become abject. "Don't kill me. Just take the Head and go. Please don't kill me."

The woman seemed to be unaware that he had even spoken. She was looking past Byron, past even the louvers of the window. Byron was naked and on his knees. "Or if you have to kill me, then do it fast. Please don't torture me."

Still she didn't seem to have heard him. "My companions will be here very soon. In fact..."

A white Ford Bronco with dark figures within was pulling into the parking lot. The woman all but echoed the words of Ten Day Gene, except Gene had been talking about himself and she was talking to and about Byron. "The next sound you hear could well be the Fat Lady's aria."

Byron had reached that point of calm and clarity when fear gives way to certainty. "Can I ask you one thing?"

"What's that?"

"Did you have to spend the night fucking me before you brought in the butchers?"

She smiled at him almost sadly. "Of course, I did, my darling. Didn't you ever hear of the mantis syndrome?"

Written 1997, previously published in a weird Belgian magazine called Cronygan Well.

VISIONS OF A SHORT APOCALYPSE

After a couple of years in LA, I started to experience apocalyptic visions. Not that I hadn't had apocalyptic visions previously. Visions aplenty since I was a lad, but L.A. just seemed to bring them out in Technicolor and VistaVision, not to mention THX digital sound. Hollywood is just the perfect backdrop. Palm trees and the glass towers of Century City against an angry red sunset, what Jim Morrison called the "bloody red sun of fantastic L.A.", cry out for an ending. And let's not forget that industrial Hollywood is the wellspring of end-of-days fantasy. It's the company town that gave us *The Towering Inferno*, *Dr. Strangelove*, *Earth V The Flying Saucers*, *When Worlds Collide*, and it is where I learned from Don Vito Corleone that the orange was the symbol of death. And if that wasn't quite enough for an immigrant, so great and dark a culture lies to the South, but for so long suppressed, we should not be surprised that we fear earthquakes.

THE AZTEC CALENDAR JUST RAN OUT

The night is lit by the chrome-flare of falling warriors
Carrion scavengers scrabble for white hot insignia
You thought the biblical end times were a motherfucker?
Listen friend
The Aztec calendar just ran out.

Witchfire as the hotel burns
Ain't no point in saving your luggage
Ain't no point in even saving your soul
Walk the dog, baby
The Aztec calendar just ran out.

Dice roll redundant under their own power
The shooter ain't coming out ever again
The pit boss goes down on his own gun
Cops know fear
The Aztec calendar just ran out.

Passion flowers in smoldering rags
Have no pointers to salvation
Custom car cannibals put it park
The death knell is number one on the Billboard Hot
    Hundred
The Aztec calendar just ran out.

How long do you think a single species
Can go round and round in the revolving door
Without someone thinking "this shit must stop?"
The Aztec calendar just ran out.

Written 1997. Recorded with Andy Colquhoun in the same year. Released in 1998 on the CD The Deviants Have Left The Planet *on Capt. Trips Records, Tokyo.*

Just to prove that the apocalyptic vision is nothing new, the next story was written all the way back in 1973. I had thought it lost until it was unearthed by Rich Deakin who, with Phil Jones, operates the Funtopia website.

A LINE'S A LINE

Easy Willie comes through the door, a practice which he makes a habit.

"The crowd is restless."

"Unh?"

"Like cows before a thunder storm."

"Aah."

"You have no idea what I'm talking about."

"No."

"Want a logical resume of what is wrong with things?"

"No."

"That's the trouble with you."

I lie on the floor and patiently ignore him. In the gap between the window and the door the sky looks like a thin strip of nasty, pale blue virus culture. Maybe if I eat a couple more it will go away. Maybe if I eat six, Willie will go away too. I look in the box. There's only two left, plus about half a one that I'd been nibbling for half the previous day. Willie, not getting any attention, starts to fuck with the incubator.

"Don't fuck with the incubator."

"Why not?"

"The chickens'll get out."

"So?"

"They're my fucking chickens."

"That's the trouble with you."

There's no escaping Willie. The sky looks even more virulent. I sit up, get up, walk across the room. Close that last gap of curtain. Then I go to the stereo and turn down "Fat Man" by the Hawks. I look Willie straight in the eye. A cool, even, tight-lipped, high plains drifter look in the eye. Paranoid, see it through, auto destruct look.

"What's the matter with me?"

Willie shuffles in a circle like Step'n Fetchit. "Oo-we-oo. I was listening to that."

I grit my teeth, bad mescaline, cheap Scotch, Henry Fonda ragged. "What's the matter with me?"

"You're just like all the rest. Five cents, please."

Willie makes as if to go, but I grab him, wrestle him to the floor. I pick up a bottle from the corner and threaten him with it. "Tell me about it."

"You're paranoid."

"So? What else is new?"

"The human race is dying out."

"So?"

"You don't care?"

"I'll kill you, Willie."

"It's a line."

"Hunh?"

"Snurf."

"Unh?"

"Snurf."

"Whaa?"

"It's a line."

"That's one way of looking at it."

"Can I get up again?"

I don't say anything, but lie down on the floor again. Willie gets up and dusts himself off. He looks at the incubator, looks at me, looks back at the incubator. I raise my head. "I warned you."

Willie alters course and heads past the incubator and over to the window. He parts the curtains. I go white at the knuckles. I know it, I don't even have to look. "Shut those fucking curtains." The sky is overcrowded with hostile organisms looking for someone to infect. Willie reluctantly closes the curtains. I crawl to the TV. It's the *Wet Woman's Show*. A blonde with big tits is having buckets of water poured over her to the tune of "April in Paris." It isn't hard to follow and we watch it in silence for a while. Then Willie turns his head slowly. "You don't care, do you?"

"About what?"

"Got a cigarette?"

"Sure." I toss over the packet. A mild blend. "What don't I care about?"

Willie lights his cigarette just like they used to do on the commercials. "The human race is dying out."

"There's plenty of them left."

"The rats and roaches will inherit the earth."

"Nothing else?"

"Penguins. Maybe where it's cold."

"So?"

"You ought to be concerned."

"Why?"

"It's extinction time. You've seen the figures."

"Nothing I can do."

"All you want to do is snort coke off lumps of polished agate."

"I don't have no polished agate."

"You don't have no coke either."

"Is that what you came looking for?"

"No." Willie looks out of the window again. Again I yell at him. "Shut it. It gets in."

"Let's go out."

"Out?"

"Sure. Out."

"Where?"

"Under the overpass."

I begin to get agitated. Willie is starting to make me swell internally. I can feel it. I stare at the floor. I think some of the sky virus is hiding among the pile on the carpet. I look back at Willie. I'm sure he's an agent sent in to get me outside on my own. "I don't want to go out."

"Why not?"

"If the temperature drops the chickens will die."

"So?"

"They're my chickens, and, anyway, under the overpass we're quite likely to get mortally stomped by Seconal crazed juveniles."

"Rubbish, we're too big and feisty. They only pick on school girls and old people. We ain't going to get either robbed or raped."

"I don't want to go there."

"Okay, let's not go there, let's go see a fuck film."

"No!"

"Why not?"

"Those places are full of scummy old people who cough up green stuff and want to touch you."

"Suit yourself."

The sullen silence falls upon us. On TV two redheads are beating each other with celery. Celery in bilious color. Willie peers at the screen. "Want I should fuck with the colour guns?"

"No, you'll damage it."

"Who, me?"

"Yes, you. I don't trust you."

"There you go again."

"Hunh?"

"You'd think people would get a bit more excited about becoming extinct."

"Meaning me?"

"Sure, why not?"

"I don't like the human race."

"Then why aren't you jumping about?"

"It isn't like it was something good."

"Like what?"

"I don't know. Godzilla, something with class."

"The extinction of a species ain't good enough for you, then? You gotta have class. You gotta have fucking Godzilla before you'll raise a grin."

"Sure. That's what they have on *Star Trek*."

"Name one of the first men on the moon."

"Who gives a fuck?"

"You can name anyone out of *Star Trek*."

"Sure, any time."

"But you don't care about the demise of the human race?"

"Like I said, who gives a fuck? They're all fucking animals anyway."

"It's a line though."

I shrug. "If you say so."

On TV, men in black PVC suits turn fire hoses on a pit filled with two years' worth of Playmates-of-the-Month.

Written 1973. Published in the same year in IT *issue #161.*

Even today, as I stare bleakly at the world stage and its frighteningly untalented players, I continue to wonder what magical wonderland we might inhabit had JFK founded his dynasty. Jack Kennedy was the last politician in whom I found it plausible to believe, to the point that I ask myself, where might the world have been had Jack remained president for two terms? Then Bobby for two terms, and then one term of Teddy followed by a four-year Republican revival? By that time, the late John-John would have been old enough for his own coronation, in a perfect Camelot where the CIA had been cut down to size, the Vietnam War had been sidestepped, marijuana was legal, world population was being intelligently tackled, AIDS was cured if it had ever happened at all, and a manned colony had been established on Mars. Okay, so somewhere along the line, the gilded brothers might have fouled up. Nixon and J. Edgar Hoover would have still been around to cause trouble in this alternate timeline. If they did in fact order the hit on Marilyn, their karma would have tripped them. Maybe they wouldn't have managed a U.S. Utopia by 1984, but, on the other hand, they might have, and I'm allowed to dream.

ZAPRUDER'S FILM

The mass intoned to muffled drums
The child and the black horse come
In that pink halo vapored brain
A hope that never comes again
And innocence is crushed beneath
Dark shadows that deny belief

And down the years no time to kill
Zapruder's film is rolling film

And whom and why and what it tolls
Ghost gunmen on a grassy knoll
Brightday backseat Cadillac
Our passion cannot roll it back
Or edit out, rewrite the end
No golden age, no gold to lend
And down the years, no time to kill
Zapruder's film is rolling still

Head jerks forward, head jerks back
Triangulation, planned attack
Concrete basement, lips are sealed
And ruthless men have cut their deal
And we will never trust again
The public masks of ruthless men
And down the years, no time to kill
Zapruder's film is rolling still

Echoes print that awful sound
And still they violate the wounds
The king is fallen, harvest fails
We enter time of guns and jails
A lifetime and no truth unfolds
An image while the head explodes
And down the years, no time to kill
Zapruder's film is rolling still
Zapruder's film is rolling still

Written November 1993 on the thirtieth anniversary of the assassination of John Fitzgerald Kennedy. Recorded 1995 with Jack Lancaster for the CD The Deathray Tapes, *released 1995 by Alive Records, Los Angeles.*

Trains have played their crucial part in the organized slaughter of the twentieth century. Tracks were laid with precision to the death camp and the gulag and the place of reeducation. Trains took Geronimo and his Chiracowa Apache to internment. An accurate time table was needed and devised for every final solution.

STEEL RAILS

Steel rails running to the vanishing point
Polished bright by the iron wheels of a thousand freightcars
    of trains that always run on time

No doubts will be permitted to linger
And the sentimental images of families or lovers with future
    dreams
Or the rich smell of fresh laundered linen
Or of an evening meal cooking on a stove
While in another room children listen to clowns and
    singers
On an upright radio but these will have no place in the
    order
No position in the universal mechanism

All perceptions will harden
Forged in the black and red consuming fire of absolute
    manifest certainty
As, with a vision of utopia, we join the lockstep of the heart
    and mind
Clear in our thinking that such as they are beneath
    contempt
And, in their failure to accept the new Jerusalem, their
    degeneracy will be confirmed
We are constructing the machine
We are already laying the tracks

Steel rails running to the vanishing point
Polished bright by the iron wheels of a thousand freightcars
    of trains that always run on time

All fleeting unease at the reality of what we do will be buried
    by elemental brute insistence
Drowned by the cacophony of bugles and the motor pulse
    of marching drums
And even the last lingering stench of death eliminated by
    the abstract clerical purity
Of lists and ledgers, documentation and schedule
And, in the timetable perfection, the poet will compose
    patriot worksongs
For the crews who level the forest and grade the roadbed

Steel rails running to the vanishing point
Polished bright by the iron wheels of a thousand freightcars
    of trains that always run on time

Fixed and infinite, the machinery will self-sustain perpetual
    motion for a thousand years
Straightened and strengthened by an anthill order and a
    structured hate
And the panorama in the flames of destiny's barbaric
    furnace
For, if not, we would surely fall to weakness
Look down and we would surely fall to weakness
Look away and we would surely fall
We would surely fall to our knees beside the tracks
And, bent double in horror, beat our own foreheads to
    bloody shame
On those selfsame steel rails

Written 1999, never previously published.

The thought is hardly original, but it does

not negate that a great many of the problems of humanity, maybe the majority, are a result of the sure and certain foreknowledge of the inevitability of our own deaths. Such awareness is the basis of all religion and much philosophy; what Bill Burroughs used to call "the Immortality Racket." On a much more fundamental level, the cognizance of our extreme transience is the root of the need to leave a mark. The need is felt by scientists and soldiers, poets and politicians, artists and architects. Some without the required talent or job skills looked to short-cut the process and make their mark through murder. The basic principle was that of, when you went, you took as many of the sons of bitches with you as you could. Each man was ever at war with the rest of his species.

Once a simple suicide was enough to be noticed. Jumpers waited atop tall buildings for a crowd to gather before they jumped. Then Charles Whitman had a better idea on his Texas tower. He took some guns with him and started picking off those below. From that point on, if you wanted pictures at eleven, you had to go one better than the last poor homicidal bastard. The constant challenge to the seer of apocalyptic visions is to simply keep up. Chapman and Hinkley shot celebrities, Kleebold and Harris tried to take out the high school. As the horror escalates, it was only possible to take a sample level of aberration and freeze it.

THE DISGRUNTLED EMPLOYEE

I have an AR15//And four boxes//Of two twenty three//High velocity hollow points//And I have quite a lot of Demerol// Left over from my hernia surgery//And a pint of Hiram Walker's ten high//
So I will feel no pain//When the shooting starts

And I am going to the plant tomorrow morning
To waste as many of the sons of bitches as I can
Before they waste me
I am the disgruntled employee
I am the new face of labour relations

Since they broke the union//We've taken three pay cuts//And given up the productivity bonus//And half the medical plan//And after Darlene left//And took the kids//I started getting//Too much sugar in my diet//And too many pork products//And began//Having conversations//With the Japanese guy//Inside the TV

And I am going to the plant tomorrow morning
To waste as many of the sons of bitches as I can
Before they waste me
I am the disgruntled employee
I am the new face of labour relations

Last Friday//I spent eighty-seven dollars//Plus tax and tip//Buying dinner and Harvey Wallbangers//For Jackie Kovak//At Big Billy's Steak and Lobster Barn//Out on I-7//And afterwards//She refused to give me so much//As a handjob//Said she just wanted//Us to be friends//And the next day//I saw her//And some of the other women//From quality control//Talking and laughing//Outside the female facility//And I knew they were talking about me

And I am going to the plant tomorrow morning
To waste as many as the sons of bitches as I can
Before they waste me
I am the disgruntled employee
I am the new face of labour relations

And tomorrow night
When you get home from work
You'll see me on TV

I am the disgruntled employee

Written 1994. Recorded 1995 with Jack Lancaster for the CD The Deathray Tapes, *released 1995 by Alive Records, Los Angeles.*

While back visiting in New York City, John Collins and I happened to walk past the site on Park Avenue South that had once been Max's Kansas City, but was now a Korean grocery store. An entire world, a complete link in the chain of popular culture, had simply been wiped from the map by the forces of gentrification. I was momentarily gripped by an angry and wishful vision in which the eye-shadow dead would rise from their silver-satin graves as in an old EC Comic for The Night of the Spangled and Glittery Dead, prowl the night-streets they once owned, in their Spandex shrouds, to gnaw on the skulls of the yuppie scum who, in their greed for Starbucks and real estate had forced the whores, junkies, drag queens, and Seconal vendors out of Union Square.

RHINESTONES AND QUAALUDES

Blank partisans in a war between worlds
Fighting a foe unremembered
Hanging ten surfers froze on the curl
Iced by the winds of December

Hollowed-eyed cherubs from towns without pity
No pity themselves, they've been so abused
Zombie princesses from the back room at Max's
Still can't remember the cruelty refused

Character assassins and gangster avengers
Remembering gunfire that ruined their health
All golden victims from Rodney's lost island
Jean Genie is out there and he ain't by himself

Rhinestones and Quaaludes and white walking corpses
Unnatural acts in full view of the bar
Sweet Candy Darling and poor Johnny Thunders
Will Ziggy stop playing that fucking guitar?

Hi-ho Silver Lining, the lost are returning
Hi-ho Diamante, they're coming back fast
Hi-ho Gold Lamé, the lost are returning
Hi-ho sweet baby, watch out for your ass

They're coming down Sunset
You're hearing the drumming
They're coming, they're coming
From graves so unfair
Park Avenue South like a kiss on the mouth
They're coming, they're coming
Through Union Square
An October parade of payback is coming
Problem, solution, be there or be square

Rhinestones and Quaaludes and white walking corpses
Unnatural acts in full view of the bar
Darby Crash moaning to Bela Lugosi
Will Ziggy stop playing that fucking guitar?

Written 1992. Recorded 1996 and released 1997 by Shattered Records, Los Angeles, as part of the CD compilation Unsung.

As the twentieth century drew to a close, I attempted a summation of just five sentences.

A ROOM SOAKED IN GASOLINE

Have you noticed how many times it all basically comes down to a bunch of men sitting in a gasoline soaked room, wondering which among them is sufficiently psychotic to strike a match?

And then Ernie from Petaluma takes out his Zippo, and he snaps it once, just clicking the top, not touching the wheel. That ringing metallic ping and click. Open shut, open shut.

Hey guys
Any of you mind if I smoke?

Written 1997. Never previously published in this form.

Enter the Swordmaid

I have spent a great deal of time with the vampire Victor Renquist. Four novels worth to be precise, written and published by Tor Books between 1996 and 2002. At the start, it was only supposed to be one book, but I was having so much fun in this non-human world, and a certain neo-Gothically inclined readership seemed to enjoy the experience; the first one, *The Time Of Feasting*, grew to a whole quartet, and even then I had to return to him for another brief encounter. The four books were not, however, the start of the story. I had been fascinated by the idea of the vampire since I scared and delighted myself at the tender age of nine by reading *Dracula*. The undead had such a great life. They slept all day, were blessed with a cool black wardrobe, and, above all, were not required to die.

The character who became in this story Ophelia Dane was really the invention of the writer Natalie Nichols, and grew to its following form after a long conversation in a Hollywood diner. The girl with the paranormal sword belongs to her, and she will doubtless go on and use her in the future.

ENTER THE SWORDMAID

The Terminal Tavern, so aptly named in Renquist's estimation, was less than a block from the downtown bus station. At a distance it was nothing more than lonely red and blue Budweiser lights on an otherwise deserted street, but, as he approached, it showed all the signs of gathered and vulnerable humanity. Once inside, he found the Terminal Tavern to be exactly as he had anticipated; a threadbare and exhausted place, repeatedly repaired with gaffer tape and crude varnish, but hidden from close interior inspection by dim red lights and a country music jukebox. The bar smelled of yeast, cleaning products, and directionless and defeated humans, too long under foot. For a Nosferatu, it represented a hunting ground of last resort and tainted prey, and Victor Renquist could not resist a twinge of shame that he must, by force of expediency, lurk for his survival in such a debased location. His only excuse for so lowering himself was that, when crossing a continent in a black and sealed limousine, one must take what was readily available and move swiftly on. Not that the word swift could in any way be applied to his immediate situation. While Travis, his human driver waited in the car, in an induced and mindless, but beneficially restful trance, Renquist simply waited, like some damned house cat at a mouse-hole, unwilling to select any of the currently available prey, but ever aware of the sun's arrival in a few short hours.

Renquist's entrance had, of course, caused something of a dull stir in the Terminal Tavern. Even before the door from the street had closed behind him, heads turned, eyebrows were raised, and a tired sexual frisson gripped the slatternly and overripe woman, perched on the stool on the angle of the bar, who, up to then, had been swapping routine innuendo with the pencil-mustached and bow-tied bartender. Had Renquist been a mere human, his looks alone would have caused comment. How frequently did a tall, distinguished stranger in his apparent early forties, slim and unnaturally pale, wearing a long black overcoat that draped like a cloak, enter this wretched saloon from out of the midnight darkness? He had ordered vodka by way of cover, as cold as was possible in such a place, and then removed himself to a dark and secluded booth in the back, where he hoped that, nearly out of sight, he would also soon be out of mind.

From this position of vantage, he scanned the thoughts of the denizens of the Terminal Tavern, and found them wholly unappetizing. Blunted by alcohol and stupid from television, they did no more than wallow in their modern world, disgruntled and dissatisfied, with monkey-rage simmering beneath the surface, but conditioned and domesticated through all of their short and pathetic lives to resist letting it truly erupt in any snarling overspill of real simian fury.

The bartender and two male drunks hated him instantly and instinctively, but neither of them had an inkling that he was not of their species and effectively immortal. They were easily able to hate him just because he was from elsewhere, better dressed, better looking, and with resources and options than they could not even imagine. A pony-tailed motorcyclist, with a leather jacket, turquoise jewelry, and diluted Indian genes, had a momentary spark of intuition that Renquist might be more than he seemed, but the man was too drunk and lost-cause apathetic to expand the insight to a conscious idea or theory. Of those present, the woman talking to the bartender was his most obvious victim. She had already shown an interest in him, and to isolate her from the others would be pitifully simple, except Renquist hardly wished to talk to her, let alone enter her mind. She was resentful, loveless, and contaminated by religious unpleasantness, hopelessly believing that she had been short-changed by her god, and somehow deserved better. She habitually used peppermint schnapps and sexual debasement as an antidote to an abject and desperate loneliness, but afterwards loathed herself and those barfly men who joined her in her miserable fumbling encounters. Her aura showed blood chronically tainted with not only alcohol, but also prescription painkillers that, if he fed from her, would leave him dull and irritable. Renquist still had Travis the limo driver as a mortal hole card, but only in the worse extremity did one kill the thrall that drove, and bowing to a refined and over-selective taste did not qualify as an extremity.

Victor Renquist was reluctantly steeling himself to approach the woman, and engage her in conversation as a preamble to a rapid and deadly Nosferatu seduction when he heard the sound. It was a continuous metallic resonance, as if some unnatural steel tuning fork had been struck and then allowed to ring for impossibly long as a high wordless croon, occasionally ululating to a trill, unearthly and plainly beyond the high end of human hearing, although the part-Indian did briefly look up and frown, but then dismissed the perception as nothing more than firewater imagination. The sound was originating from somewhere outside the Terminal Tavern, but seemed to be rapidly approaching. Renquist did not immediately succumb to the egocentric temptation of assuming the strange sound was directly related to him, despite the fact that he was the only one present who seemingly could hear it, and definitely the only one with knowledge of what it might be and the possible antiquity of its origins. He had walked the Earth for too long to assume every abnormality was personal. Perhaps, under different circumstances, Renquist might have experienced alarm, or even the throat catch of fear, but he was so far from anywhere he considered home, and the situation was so random, he found himself too intrigued to be disturbed.

The door opened and a young woman entered. Now the sound filled the bar like a demanding ferrous undertone. The woman was clearly no more from this place than Renquist, another transient on a random exit from the highway. Slim, dark, and almost boyish, shag-cut dark hair fell over her pale face. She was dressed for practical drama in a black denim jacket over a frilled, piratical shirt, and narrow, calf-skin jeans. Fingerless gloves and heavy engineer boots completed the ensemble, and she carried a flat Fender bass guitar case, nearly too big for her slight frame. She might have been mistaken for one of the rock & roll fugitive kind, traveling between shows and adventures, but Renquist was certain the case concealed something other than a musical instrument.

She moved to the bar and carefully leaned the bass case against the brass foot-rail. As she ordered a gin and tonic, he attempted a scan of her mind to see how many of his first impressions might be confirmed. To his surprise, he found that, apart from a dry anticipation of the drink that was being poured, her mind was closed to him. An impenetrable barrier prevented Renquist from gleaning the slightest indication as to who or what she was, or what she might be doing in the Terminal Tavern at the far side of midnight. Her pallor was such that she could have been mistaken for Nosferatu herself, but he could see enough to be assured she was wholly human. If he applied more force, he suspected he could smash his way through the barrier, but he was aware that the inevitable physical side-effects were hardly appropriate to the environment. To have the young woman convulsing all over the floor of the Terminal Tavern would create far too many questions, and he would have to satisfy his curiosity in a less violent and invasive manner.

The bar's patrons treated the arrival of the young woman as even more of an event that Renquist's appearance in their human micro-world. The bartender did his dismal best to look suave, and the other males contorted their faces into grotesque expressions that Renquist, without probing, assumed was each one's idea of looking his best. Of all of them, the motorcyclist was the most bold. He half rose from his stool. "Yo, baby, come over and join us."

The woman looked at him coldly and shook her head. "Thanks all the same, but I've been driving all night. I just need to sit and chill for a while."

"So chill with us boys."

"I don't think so."

She picked up her guitar case and drink and began walking calmly to a booth, and, by default, directly towards Renquist, who, despite his Nosferatu detachment, found himself impressed by the way she moved and handled herself. She seemed so fully in control, and while balancing the full glass and the weight of the case, still managed to demonstrate a tough, if weary, self-assurance that he could only admire, particularly as he was certain her outward confidence was a shield against a deeper vulnerability. The motorcyclist chose the same moment to show himself unwilling to take no for an answer. "What's the matter, sweet thing? You too good to drink with the likes of us?"

The young woman half turned, but did not put down her case. "Give me a break, okay? I'm tired and I just stopped in for a quiet drink."

For a second, Renquist though he might have to intervene on her behalf, but her bleak-diamond stare stopped the oaf in his tracks, and the bartender did the rest. "Quit bothering the customers, Nelson. You know the rules. You wanna be eighty-sixed again?"

The motorcyclist shrugged and returned to his stool with only a token protest. "Shit, Mo, I was only being hospitable."

Renquist allowed the girl a few minutes to settle, drink, and gather herself, before he rose to his feet and approached her booth, hoping he did not too much resemble the opportunist biker. "I haven't heard a sound like that in centuries."

The woman looked up. She had not been aware of Renquist's soft, undead closeness, but only the slightest intake of breath betrayed her surprise. Beyond that, she stared at him with a cooly measured outward caution. "Sound?"

"I haven't heard a sword singing in a very long time."

She smiled ruefully and with resignation. "You're not one of the local hillbillies are you?"

Renquist also smiled and shook his head, radiating all the non-threatening charm he could muster. "No. I am a traveler like yourself. My name is Victor Renquist."

"Ophelia Dane."

"I'm happy to meet you.

Renquist offered his hand, and after a slight hesitation, she took it and shook it, but then frowned uncertainly. "Your hand is ice cold."

"An occupational hazard."

"And what occupation is that?"

"Some think of me as an historian."

She did nothing to disguise her disbelief. "And that's how you were aware of the swordsong?"

"In part."

"Perhaps you'd better sit down, Victor Renquist. It would seem we have a mutual enigma going on here."

As Renquist folded into Ophelia Dane's booth, the men at the bar watched sullenly. This was only to be expected, but Renquist did not have to concern himself with human jealousies. At the same time, however, the note of the sword changed. Now it sounded edgy, unhappy, perhaps dangerous. "Your sword doesn't like me?"

"My sword doesn't like anyone. It's territorial, very protective, and leans to being petulant. Ignore it and it'll quiet down."

"I would guess your sword has a name."

Ophelia Dane laughed. Who was Renquist trying to fool? "If you know that much, you also know that I wouldn't tell you the name except under the most extreme circumstances." Her face hardened. "Why don't we cut the crap, Victor Renquist? What are you, and what do you want?"

"You're very direct."

"I have to be. The world I inhabit can be one of great and sudden peril."

She spoke with such grim certainty, Renquist totally believed her. "In answer to your second question, I am only curious about this chance encounter. I want nothing."

"Really?"

"Really."

"And my first question? What of that? Will you tell me what are you?"

"I'm not sure you would believe me if I told you."

A trace of scorn tightened the corners of Ophelia's mouth. "I have seen a great deal since the sword came to me, Mr. Renquist."

"I can imagine."

She flexed the fingers of her right hand, as though easing a chronic tension. "So?"

"Secrets can carry a great weight of responsibility."

"You know about my sword."

"I part recognized and part guessed the nature of your sword. You didn't burden me with the knowledge." He gestured to the Fender case that she had protectively placed between herself and the wall. "I take it the sword travels in there."

"You're avoiding the issue."

Renquist scrutinized the young woman's face. "You ask what I am?" One of his most inflexible rules was never to reveal his true nature to a human, unless absolutely and unavoidably necessary. He could rationalize that the ownership of a singing, sentient blade put Ophelia Dane well beyond the realm of normal humanity, but he knew that he was considering trusting her with the truth simply as a tactic to learn more about this strange and supposedly magical sword. As a breach of his self-imposed code, the trade was hardly ethical, but his curiosity pushed him hard.

"I am Nosferatu."

For long hanging seconds she stared at him without speaking. The sword was suddenly silent, and lights in the Terminal Tavern seemed to lose their color and become leeched and brittle. Renquist noticed a small dragon pendant hung from her neck on a short silver chain. When Ophelia Dane spoke she chose her words with care. "I knew in theory that your kind existed, but I never thought I'd ever come face to face with one of you."

"I don't mean the stuff of legend, cheap films and fiction."

"Neither do I." Ophelia now made direct eye contact with Renquist. Her gaze didn't waver. "And if you're planning to make me your victim, I must warn you that I don't kill easily."

Renquist shook his head and smiled. He supposed it was a natural reaction for a human, no matter how distanced she might be from her own kind, but feeding from her had been the very last thing on his mind. Prey came easily, but a true swordmaiden, if in fact she was one, was a rarity, a mystery, and too unique to be used up in mundane blood-letting. "Believe me, I have no intention of harming you."

"I have your word on that?"

"You have my word on that."

The encased sword emitted a brief trill, and Ophelia was momentarily distracted. He mind was still closed to Renquist, but he was sure that the mysterious weapon had spoken to her, and she in turn had understood. Renquist tried for confirmation of his guess with a shot in the dark. "The sword doesn't trust my word?"

Ophelia only faltered for the briefest of moments, but it was all that Renquist needed. He required no further indication that Ms. Dane and the sword could converse without him being aware of what passed between them, and such a capability had to put him at a potential disadvantage. She recovered so quickly that a mortal would have hardly noticed. "As I already told you, my sword is also my protector. It distrusts everyone and everything until it is assured otherwise."

In a human, such speed of reaction was usually a sign that, at some point in the past, they had been subject to a training regime that was both lengthy and rigorous, but Renquist let slip no sign of his observation, and kept the conversation obliquely trivial. "A useful companion."

Ophelia permitted herself an arch smile, pre-relishing her own humor. "It's always a…double-edged blessing. It has its ways and idiosyncracies."

Renquist dutifully laughed. "I have known a great many swords in my time."

"I don't doubt that. If it's not an impolite question, exactly how long is your time?"

"Again you would not believe me."

"Try me."

Renquist paused a moment for shameless dramatic effect. "I became what I am in the twelfth century of this so-called Christian era."

"Good god."

"No god was involved."

"You are almost a thousand years old?"

"I said you wouldn't believe me."

"Oh, I believe you. I'm already sitting in a run-down, provincial gin mill with a vampire, so what's not to believe?"

Renquist's face hardened. "We don't use that word. We Nosferatu consider it pejorative."

"I'm sorry."

"You couldn't have known."

"Please go on telling me about your swords."

"Right now I carry a sixteenth century bushido blade. It was given to me by Hideo Matsutani, the great undead swordsman of Kyoto." Ophelia said nothing, so Renquist continued. His plan was to calm any remaining fears on her part by talking swords like the expert he was. "It had the unfortunate reputation of being what the sixteenth century Japanese called an "evil blade." After a failed uprising against a particularly despotic human shogun, it was used by its previous owner when he assisted in the ritual suicides of three of his friends and co-conspirators."

"He didn't kill himself?"

"Only after he had dispatched his companions. Then he formally handed it to a fourth knight who had used it on him. Perversely, it seems to have changed its character since coming into my care."

"But it doesn't sing?"

"No, it doesn't sing, but at times I fancy I hear an elusive metallic purring."

Ophelia's expression became just the slightest fraction flirtatious. "I would like to hear your bushido purr."

Renquist spread his hands as though in proof that he was unarmed. "Alas, I don't carry the Matsutani blade with me in places like this."

"I suppose you are curious to see my companion."

"Of course. A singing sword is a rare object, but I would hardly be so gauche as to come out and ask."

"The question is can I trust you?" The sword made a muffled interjection, and Ophelia grimaced as if it was telling her something she did not want to hear. Maybe the sword objected to being displayed like an exhibit. Or perhaps it and Ophelia had just conceived an agenda of their own.

Renquist allowed her a moment to refuse him, but he was

certain that her bold competitiveness would force her to show, if not tell. "If you have misgivings, I wouldn't dream of imposing."

Ophelia glanced round. "Not in here. We would have to go somewhere."

Renquist was disinclined to suggest that they take the sword to his limousine. Part of him wavered at the idea out of pure self protection. She could too easily read the license plate, and identify him in the future. He also feared she might spook at entering such an enclosed and private space with him. "Where would you suggest?"

"I suppose we could go out to my car."

Renquist didn't immediately answer. "Your car?"

With this pantomime of unstated doubt, Renquist had effectively turned the tables of misgiving on Ophelia. Now she pressed the point, treating the revelation of her weapon as a challenge. "Yes, my car. My classic '68 Roadrunner, no less. You have a problem with that?"

"No problem I can think of."

She grasped the handle of the Fender case. "Then shall we?"

"Why not?"

The open air of the street seemed clean and clear after the interior of the Terminal Tavern. Just as Ophelia had claimed, an immaculate, dark green Roadrunner stood an aloof distance from two pick-ups, a Harley Davidson Electroglide, a Cutlass Supreme, and a dented Honda Civic with Republican Party and Fundamentalist Christian bumper stickers and decals, that stood flocked together, and were presumably the collected transportation of Mo and his customers. Ophelia took the lead and Renquist, after a single backward glance, followed. "I imagine a sexual connotation will be put on our leaving like that."

"Who gives a fuck what a bunch of drunks think?" Ophelia reached the car and gently placed the Fender case on the hood, plainly respecting both the sensitivity of the sword and the hand-rubbed finish of the car. Before she snapped back the locks, she looked at Renquist. "I hope you'll behave yourself. I would hate to raise a cross to you."

"A cross would do you no good. It's nothing but a human superstition."

Ophelia opened the fastenings on the case, but Renquist halted and lifted a hand in silent warning. He had heard a movement from inside the bar, undetectable to Ophelia's ears. The door opened and Nelson, the part-Indian motorcyclist, lurched out. His drunken intention was to follow Renquist and Ophelia Dane, in the hope of catching them in some variety of carnal disarray. What he meant to do after that was unclear to both him and Renquist, but since it was not to be allowed, it hardly mattered. Renquist needed to conjure no hell-vision to get rid of the man. The projected suggestion that it was a very bad idea for Nelson to be under the open sky was more than enough to make the motorcyclist gasp and reel back into the Terminal Tavern.

Ophelia blinked. "How did you do that?"

Renquist looked implausibly modest. "Control of humans is absurdly easy."

Ophelia seemed about to say something to the effect that she too was human, but then decided to assert her own equality of power by simply opening the case and exposing her blade. No debate; Renquist was so impressed, he all but stared transfixed. Just on its own, the faint aura-shimmer that rose from the case as the top was lifted told him he was not dealing with any simple forging of lifeless metal. The weapon was a sentient thing, self-aware, and even by Renquist's expansive standards of normality, very, very strange. How had Ophelia Dane come by such a thing, and what task, quest or mission was her doom or destiny now she bore it? The sword itself was in no way as Renquist had imagined it. He had expected something hallowed and ancient, hatched by ages of combat, but the blade appeared newly forged and freshly appointed. Renquist was no metallurgist, but he would have wagered odds that the steel was some advanced tungsten alloy, with molecules scarcely cooled from the furnaces of Pittsburgh, Sheffield, or the Ruhr. Casual inspection showed it to be a simple, two-edged broadsword with a central gutter and a simple cross-guard. The hilt was bound in dark red lizard skin and crowned with a modestly fluted counter-weight. No frills, gems, or curlicues had been added to impede its deadly practicality of purpose, and the very modernity of its design ensured that it was light and easily handled even by one as small of stature as Ophelia.

Renquist was awed. "How did you come by such a wonder?"

"That's a long story."

"I imagined it would be.

"Suffice to say the sword is not entirely of this world."

Renquist treated her to a sideways glance. "Not of this world?"

"To be more precise, not of this dimension's reality."

He experienced the faintest of chills. When it came to the inter-dimensional, Nosferatu were as helpless, uninformed, and vulnerable as any flesh and blood man or woman. He nursed a bitter recall of his conflict with the dire Cthulhu, which had all but ended in his destruction and true death, and had left him in no doubt that the undead, powerful as they might be in their own world, had no business in the multi-dimensional and extra-human universe that lay only crucial microns and nanoseconds away.

"Pick it up if you like. Feel the balance and heft of it."

Now Renquist's reluctance was genuine, no tactical ploy. The sword was humming and did not sound happy to his ear. He was far from sure that he wanted to touch it. If all that had happened so far was just bait in an elaborately set trap, the logical moment for the surprise to be sprung was when he touched the sword. On the other hand, he had to know more, and no aphorism about cats, curiosity, and death need apply.

Ophelia must have sensed his caution. "Pick it up, Renquist. But don't perform any overly flamboyant maneuvers. The sword may not be altogether happy. It probably sees you as an invasion of our mutual symbiosis, and if you start swinging it around like *Zorro Rides Again*, it could all too readily freak out and put the zap on your head."

She was challenging him again, but her words actually afforded him more space for delay. "You and the sword are symbiotes?"

"That's what I was taught. We both gain from the energy released at the death of an adversary. But you should know all about that. Isn't death-energy the key to the undead metabolism?"

"I am not a great believer in death-energy physics."

"No? I heard the blood you take is really only symbolic."

Renquist shook his head. "The blood is definitely not symbolic. Believe me. If it was, I'd be an Episcopalian."

Ophelia did not seem to get Renquist's obscure blood-as-a-symbol jest, and began to show signs of impatience. "I though you wanted to try the sword?"

"I do."

With his retreat effectively cut off by a possible loss of face, he placed his hand on the hilt and lifted the weapon from the crushed velvet interior of the case. Normally shaped to accommodate a Fender Precision Bass, the protective blocking of the case had been custom remodeled to the outline of the sword. A tooled and silver-mounted leather sheath rested in a separate recess. Seemingly the blade traveled naked, although Renquist had no idea why. He stepped back from the car and raised the weapon, testing its weight, relieved that nothing untoward had occurred on first contact, and the sword remained mute as he gripped it. He swung it gently and, as he had expected, it handled beautifully. Even allowing for his Nosferatu strength, an uncanny lightness suggested it contributed its own power to that of the arm that wielded it. With growing confidence, he swung the sword a little more forcefully. The sword began quietly to hum, but Renquist could feel no vibration to his hand or arm, and no sense of the blade being angry or displeased. Succumbing to a temptation to show off, he pivoted gracefully on the balls of his feet and swung again, left and right.

The shock hit him like a massive jolt of electricity. He knew in the very juncture of flash and pain, that so far the sword had been playing with him; seducing him with its light and effortless performance. Now it had him. Renquist was helpless. His right hand was paralyzed clear to the elbow, and, try as he might, he could not let go his grip on the hilt. Worse still, the world he'd inhabited a second before had vanished. The parking lot was gone, Ophelia and her green car were gone. He could no longer see the lights of the Terminal Tavern. As Ophelia had predicted, the sword had turned and indeed put the zap on Renquist's head. He was in a place without perspective or solid form. Flowing psychedelics of other dimensions, bright, colorful, but completely insubstantial, swirled and spiraled around him. A chanting murmur of alien voices, indistinct and unintelligible, but amplified to the threshold of pain, hammered in his head. Renquist recognized it all as the approach of madness, but he knew he must not submit or yield. Without knowing whether the experience was real or virtual, he slowed his breathing and willed back the pain that threatened to drown him.

A loud and imperial voice cut through the arrhythmic but percussive moan of chaos. "*He's undead and should be slain for the general good.*"

He thought he heard other voices protesting the spoken edict, but he wasn't sure, drowned as they were in the general cacophony, but even the semblance of debate over his slaying was of some comfort. Comfort, however, was short-lived. Invisible tremors shook his already tenuous physical perception, and the turmoil around him darkened, as though formless clouds were gathering to extinguish all light. An evil-howling wind snatched at him, and aggressive fear stabbed like a frozen dagger. The voice spoke again. "*Is this the onset of your true death, Victor Renquist?*"

Dark shapes like the silhouettes of armed men closed around him, and Renquist was all but smothered by the stench of a battlefield. The air was heavy with berserker howling, cries, death groans, and the clash of arms. In a forked lightning flash of clarity, fell figures on tall, black, iron-shod horses thundered past him. The sword of Ophelia appeared, a white-blazing beacon in the roiling murk, sharp and clear, in total contrast to the immaterial shade who wielded it, wildly hacking at equally disembodied foes. Then, in another black-night electric storm-crash, he again saw clearly; warrior swordsmen, and foot-soldiers with pike and spear, faces hidden behind the masks of horned iron helmets, slipping and scrambling in a knee-deep, sucking mire of gore and crushed stone, slain flesh, churned mud, and feces that caked their armor and slowed their movements as they fought desperately not to fall before the lances of the cavalry. High above the combatants were aura-hints and mind-traces of ancient, tentacled, squid-like things that both directed and relished the carnage. And Ophelia was there in the thick of the slaughter, hair matted and wet, chainmail slick with the blood of others, defending a tattered and unrecognizable banner. She seemed to be shouting to him, trying to communicate before the vision was extinguished. *"Renquist, the sword cannot be in two places at once."*

Renquist realized that this was an absolute and essential truth. The same sword that Ophelia wielded was also clutched in his own immobilized right hand. He concentrated, calling up all the power at his disposal and bringing it to bear on his own compromised body, forcing muscles and sinews to respond to the commands of his mind. The same right arm had taken practiced control of countless swords over the millennium of his undead existence. The strength and skill of his right arm had defeated a thousand enemies, and that it should fail him now was unthinkable. He could feel his spine involuntarily arch and his face contort with monstrous Nosferatu effort, but the power that held him was slowly forced back. His grip on Ophelia's living sword actually shifted. He could feel his fingers again. He was prevailing, and his first impulse was to hurl the thing from him. Then a second and more realistic logic asserted itself. He had never won a fight by throwing down the weapon, and with that thought his surroundings immediately changed. He saw the nebulous darkness coagulate into a single form. Suddenly he was back on the parking lot. The green Roadrunner gleamed and Ophelia stood beside it, but between him and the Terminal Tavern, an absolute gulf loomed, a hideous void leading to an unnamed elsewhere that Renquist could only, and very inadequately, describe as a rend in reality. Somehow, in his struggle with the sword, and the hallucinations with which it had filled his mind, either he or it had caused damage to the inter-dimensional fabric, and a vast dark thing was forcing its way through. Renquist couldn't be sure if this creature was bird, reptile, or something else entirely. It was fabricated from the pure essence of hate and eternal night, and it came at him with beak, talons, and red, baleful eyes. He ducked and spun, as projectile feathers targeted him like bolts from a crossbow. He closed with the thing, swinging the sword in a grim slashing defense, but the sword refused to perform and became a dead and sullen, unresponsive weight. He heard Ophelia scream as a razor-edged yellow claw slashed within a half inch of his face.

"Renquist! Throw me the sword! It loves me, and it will serve me!"

With no thought of pride or saving face, Renquist tossed the sword so Ophelia could deftly catch it. She immediately went at the thing in calculated offense. Sword and woman fought in matched and perfect harmony, pressing home the attack as the overjoyed and now melodically howling blade sliced easily into what passed for monster flesh. Ophelia's moves were elegant, at times balletic, never giving ground, always pressing forward, despite the thing's overwhelming size and all of its efforts to dominate the encounter. Renquist realized that Ophelia so had the measure of the inter-dimensional horror, she was actually able to take the time to show off for him, and he could only be impressed. As the blade flashed, her body moved with such grace and precision, and her cuts and lunges were delivered with such unerring speed that he was hard pressed to remember, or even believe, she was only human. In what seemed like just seconds of deceptively telescoped time, she thrust her sword-point deep into the monster's body. It let out a scream that should have woken the entire hick town, although, like the song of the sword, Renquist guessed that only he and Ophelia heard it.

The creature-from-beyond vanished, folding in on itself like dissipating smoke, and the rent fabric closed without sign of a seam. All that remained to evidence anything had happened there at all was Ophelia, leaning on her sword, catching her breath. She pushed her hair out of her eyes and smiled. She seemed about to say something when the two of them were bathed in blinding light, and a voice grated from a loudspeaker.

"Remain exactly where you are!"

Renquist's reactions faltered for a fraction of second. Still enveloped in the preceding events, he had totally forgotten the mundane human world, and could only assume this was a second intrusion from beyond. Then the sight of red and blue pulses behind the primary white-light glare, and the sound of distorted human radio crackle told him that what they now faced was nothing more than a real-world police cruiser, responding, in all likelihood, to a 51-50, the dispatchers' code for a incident involving the criminally insane. Some citizen had probably filed a report of a mad woman with a sword on the parking lot of the bar.

"Drop your weapons and get down on the ground!"

If Renquist looked past the light, he could see the crouched figures behind the open doors of the police car, and the barrels of the Glock 9mm automatic and the Mossberg pump shotgun that were leveled at him and Ophelia. For Renquist this constituted the equivalent of a last straw, and he was hard-pressed not to release a furious and unrestrained psychic assault on these provincial policemen. Only a shredded common sense, and the realization that where one cop came, backup would inevitably follow, caused him to bridle his anger. He saw no reason, though, to let these intruders down too lightly. They had startled him, they constituted a unneeded inconvenience, and for that they would suffer. Without mystic sign or physical movement, he lifted the two men by the scruffs of their human stupidity and forced them through an approximate and unfocused memory of the horror to which he himself had been so recently exposed. For a tiny fragment of time, they too were on that blood-soaked killing field in another dimension. He crowned the vision of terror with a single, simple but irresistible command. Escape from the ghastly ghost world in which they found themselves would only be achieved by climbing into their flashing cruiser, and driving like the proverbial bat out of Hades, with the siren screaming, until they were at least ten miles away. Only then would they be permitted to stop, to forget all that had so recently befallen them, and emerge from the experience wondering what the hell happened and how they would explain it.

Parking lot gravel flew in angry arcs as the driver threw the car into reverse, executed a skidding, backward turn of pure panic and then rocketed away with all the hammer-down acceleration he could thrash from the engine. Renquist only turned to Ophelia when the lights were gone and the racket of the siren was fading. She looked so apprehensive of his possible retribution that Renquist couldn't help but be amused. "I imagine you will think twice before you reveal your sword to another itinerant Nosferatu."

Ophelia Dane took a deep breath. "In all the gin joints in all the world..."

"That's one way of putting it."

"Are all your nights like this?"

Renquist shook his head and smiled. "Indeed not. Some are really eventful."

"You're joking, right?"

Renquist nodded, feeling an odd fondness for this strange and paranormally driven human. "Yes, my dear Ophelia, I'm joking."

Ophelia looked down at the sword, now quite mute. "I didn't know it would act up so badly."

"It did not take kindly to the hand of the Nosferatu."

"It's unforgivably pleased with itself."

"Put it back in its box, and remonstrate with it later, if such a thing is possible."

Without another word she did as he instructed. When the Fender case was firmly locked, she turned and faced Renquist. "Victor, I..."

He shook his head sadly. "There's nothing to be said, my dear. We had both better leave here as fast as possible. We have created enough psychic overspill to give the entire sleeping town nightmares. Many will wake and wonder."

Ophelia so obviously had a hundred questions that he though she might insist they remain, but she turned and reluctantly opened the door of the car. She placed the case in the back, then slid behind the wheel, and started the Roadrunner's engine. She let it run for a short while, then slipped the car into gear, and let out the clutch. Renquist watched her depart down the street and make the first right turn beyond the bus station. He briefly closed his eyes. Farewell, Ophelia Dane. He was tired and he still had not fed, but he was not going to feed in this town. He started walking to where the limousine was concealed. He would ignore his hunger and sleep in sealed darkness while Travis drove through the day. He would stop again and hunt only in a city where no singular and unnatural paths demanded that he cross them.

Written 2002. Never previously published.

Apocalypse More

The visions never go away. CNN seems to make sure of that.

THE EAST IS RED

We must hurry
We can waste no more time
We must leave right now or we will never leave at all
To make ourselves invisible is the only priority

Already
In the darkness before dawn, locust formations of electric
    planes
Move in the direction of the inevitable sun
And, closer to the ground, predator cruisers clear the streets
Reshaping this promised land in the uniform image
Of their ordered mechanism

Remove your dark glasses, my love, and look behind you
The east is red
Is it a new morning?
The new day dawning?
As the prophecy foretold?
Or is it just another city, once again on fire?

We must hurry or we will be taken like the others

Just two more of the usual suspects
The boom is lowered
The net is down
The airstrip is closed
And soon there will be roadblocks on the highway

Already
Fractal patterns are forming at the ocean horizon
The automatons have engaged the terminal sequence
And time has been rendered finite by the opening of the
    Masterlock
The trees of Eden wither and dire warnings are etched in
    fields

So set aside your gloves and fan, my love, and look behind
    you
Is it a new morning?
The new day dawning?
As the prophecy foretold?
Or is it just another city
Once again on fire?

We must hurry
Speed is of the essence
Schedules are now non-negotiable and time is no longer on
    our side
Concealment is impossible and flight is the only remaining
    option

Already
The waveforms have randomized
The gypsies are checking out of the Bonaventure
And only dogs know what is really happening
Although they still maintain a life of their own
The Atomic Boogie hour is off the air and Doctor Rock has
    ceased transmission
The Fat Boy now runs critical, mouth ballistic
White noise falls on dead air and reruns will no longer

suffice

So gather up your chemicals, my love, and look behind you
The east is red
Is it a new morning?
The new day dawning?
As the prophecy foretold
Or is it just another city
Once again on fire?

Written 1995. Recorded 1996 and released 1997 by Shattered Records, Los Angeles, as part of the compilation Unsung.

When I first arrived in L.A. I read a whole lot of James Elroy just to get my bearings. I hardly needed to investigate the legends of Charlie Manson and his kin. I'd done that research right along with Ed Sanders, Vince Bugliosi and the ever-Keystone LAPD, although new information did regularly surface, but all too often it related to the part played by the chicken-headed god Abraxas. I did briefly check out the Satanic Richard Ramirez, and more particularly the necrophile women who were fighting over which of them was his jailhouse fiancé, and I boned up on the mob hits called by Micky Cohen and Johnny Stompanato. In the meantime the Axl Rose boys and vacuum blondes still vanished from the funky boulevard and nobody missed them. All that was before O.J. Simpson swamped the true crime receptors for almost two years straight, but fortunately the poem was written before that obsession had to be avoided, and while Mickey and Mallory Knox were just a gleam in Oliver Stone's eye.

I believe all the slaughter is really a by-product

of the Westward-Ho migration, and the Yellow Brick Road to Hollywood, as described by both Judy Garland and Captain Beefheart. Some come seeking fame and fortune, while others simply reach the edge of the Pacific Ocean, and therefore the edge of the world, and find they can go no further because their instincts have no capacity to backtrack. Since Jack the Ripper got all that ink, and as every disgruntled employee knows, murder is the final fling at celebrity or bust.

DEAD MOVIE STARS

She'd been lost on Sunset and found in a dumpster
On Western Avenue
Dead in the manner that the living would never envy
One red shoe missing and the gold dress all ripped up
And something weird
Written across her stomach with her own lipstick

She'd been toxic drunk
When she met the guy
With the soft Woody Harrelson smile
And the homicide eyes
Only beat coke and bike queen amphetamine
Were keeping her vertical
When she accepted
His offer of a hundred
And stepped into his van

Word on the street was that the cops had him for two
   hours
Later the same night on a traffic beef
But they let him go

She'd done a walk-on in *Married With Children,*
And a *900 Heat* commercial

So maybe you could stretch things
And call her a movie star
But isn't everyone a dead movie star at Sunset and
    Western

He couldn't handle the voices in his head no more
The ones who sounded like Shelley Winters and E. Emmett
    Walsh
And all of the desperate things they wanted him to do

And on Saturday nights,
He would call the TV shrink on the eerie,
Late night
Call-in show

At first, he just dialed the number and hung up
But even when he finally brought himself to speak
He couldn't tell the TV shrink about the voices
And all the dark and terrible things they said

Or even that he was an officer
In the Los Angeles Police Department

The TV shrink
Seemed to think
It was something to do
With his wanting to fuck his mother
But that wasn't the case at all

And even the fifth of scotch and the forty Seconal
Didn't stop the voices
In fact
The sons of bitches kept right on talking at him
And talking at him
And talking at him
And talking at him
All the way to the final fade

Talking at him
About the woman in the gold dress
And the things that he had done to her

E. Emmett Walsh had wanted him
To blow his brains out in his car
On the freeway
In the rush hour
"You get on TV that way
You'll be a goddamned movie star"

But isn't everyone a dead movie star
In a black and white

First written 1992, revised a couple of times, finally recorded in a shorter form by Wayne Kramer in 1996 for the album Dangerous Madness, *Epitaph Records, Los Angeles.*

Los Angeles summer nights are never as overtly brutal as the dark of the dog days in New York City, but the brutality is really only a matter of degree and twenty percentage points of humidity. When Manhattan wilts dripping in August, and the rats desert for the Hamptons, a bad night in the Valley pulses with an arid petrochemical dementia all of its own; the kind that makes you move the TV and the AC into the bedroom, but still you dream of dry gulches. Like Dennis Hopper remarked in *Apocalypse Now*, "This is the way the world ends, man, and, with a whimper, I'm fucking splitting."

A LONG DRY SEASON

It was a long dry season and we prayed to make it to the
rains

By the third week, normal sleep had all but become impossible
And, by the fourth, the river was no more than
A sluggish trickle between baking flats of moonscape mud
Dry coughing in dust storms raised by exhausted, brick oven winds
And as the TV gave up the pretense that anything was any more right in the world
Locust cowboys and coyote warriors moved in from the hills
Desperate for a drink
Looking to slake throats of parched and cracked, tooled and studded leather
With the unholy rotgut mescal of the worm

It was a long dry season and we prayed to make it to the rains

Domestic dogs organized in packs
Feeling no longer beholden to their former masters
While green death and pallid yellow aurora arced at night
Over lovers locked and loaded
With the madness of disease taken in substitute for passion
And that would ultimately end in gunfire heard for miles
As sound that carried to infinity in the alkaline air
Across the flatlands and desiccated towns
Like Gene Autry singing someplace out beyond the Gates of Eden

It was a long dry season and we prayed to make it to the rains

High wynding howling of evaporated destiny and melted insulation
Under stars without mercy or even interest
While white foam fungoid puffballs drifted from a perpetually cloudless sky
Like snowballs from hell in the red desert Martian heated quiet
Fragmenting as they struck the hard parched earth

Powering to a diaphanous dust that crept and clung
To the electromagnetic static of relentless commercial appliances
Now wholly unwatched by women with blank purple eyes
And yucca flowers in their hair
Who murmured in dreams of reflecting pools and crystal
    fountains
And men who searched for the impossibility
Of a cool place on the pillow
To the constant drone of a mosquito fan
Only to find themselves thirst transfixed by the Doombeam
In the hands of an apparition of Captain America

It was a long dry season and we prayed to make it to the rains

Written 1997. Recorded for the Deviants' CD, Dr Crow,
released by Track Records in September 2002.

    And when the end finally comes, will there be one
left to scream the last defiant and swashbuckling
communiqué?

THE BLACK ATTACK SHIPS OF ZETA RETICULI HAVE
NOW BROKEN THROUGH THE GREAT DOUBLE
HELIX. REDLINE THE DEATHRAY, BOYS, AND PASS
THE WILD TURKEY, NOW'S THE TIME FOR THE BLAZE
OF GLORY

ACTIVATE THE AUDIO RECORD FOR THE BENEFIT
OF FUTURE HISTORIANS. AND NEVER LET IT BE
SAID THAT HOMO SAPIENS SOLD THEIR PLANET
CHEAPLY

*Written 1995. Recorded 1996 with deviants xvvi as a hidden
track for the CD* Eating Jello With A Heated Fork, *released
1996 by Alive Records, Los Angeles.*

Encore

When I was around six or seven years old we had a game that involved attempting to eat Jello (in England we called it "jelly") with knitting needles. This is an extension of the same patently absurd and dangerous idea.

EATING JELLO WITH A HEATED FORK

Eating Jello with a heated fork
The slide will get you nowhere, the green is always elsewhere
Ease of penetration, to a cancelled destination
Gravity is proved, the Jello never moved
Eating Jello with a heated fork

Written 1995. Recorded 1996 with deviants xvvi for the CD Eating Jello With A Heated Fork, *released 1996 by Alive Records, Los Angeles.*

Mick Farren was born in England on a wet night at the end of World War II. His working life has been divided between music and literature, with certain digressions into psychedelic agitprop. An endless stream of science fiction, poetry and neo-gothic novels, plus the occasional work of non-fiction, flows from his computer, as well as CDs of his music and poetry, usually with his floating rock & roll crap-game, The Deviants. His best know works are *The DNA Cowboys* trilogy, *The Renquist Quartet*, *The Black Leather Jacket*, the autobiographic *Give The Anarchist A Cigarette*. His produced plays include *A Criminal Sorority*, and the off-Broadway musical *The Last Words Of Dutch Schultz*. As a lyricist, Mick's words have been sung by Metallica, Motorhead, Hawkwind, Brother Wayne Kramer, the Royal Crown Revue, and the Pink Fairies. He currently lives in Hollywood, California and on the internet at http://doc40.blogspot.com/